DIARY OF A LOVING HEART

June Masters Bacher

HARVEST HOUSE PUBLISHERS
Eugene, Oregon 97402

DIARY OF A LOVING HEART

Copyright © 1984 by Harvest House Publishers
Eugene, Oregon 97402

Library of Congess Catalog Card Number 83-82322
ISBN 0-89081-377-9

All rights reserved. No portion of this book may be repro-
duced in any form without the written permission of the
Publisher.

Printed in the United States of America.

In loving memory
of
my father,
Jerome Kearby Masters

PREFACE

Once upon a time, a hundred years ago, only Indian trails wound in and out of Oregon's mountain-ribbed valleys. Now, buses, automobiles, and logging trucks clog the beautifully-maintained highways. Most of the occupants of the automobiles are busy, progressive Oregonians or tourists who rest travel-weary eyes on the state's eternal green. But now and then, the descendants of those "in between" generations come back for ancient-recipe apple pie, venison roasts, or a start of sourdough. It is then that they listen and relive those lovely bygone days and, ever so briefly, hear the wail of distant fiddles mingled with laughter reduced to silence, above the whisper of the pines... gently, softly, weaving a magic spell....

It is from those days that the series of pioneer-life stories in fertile valleys of the Oregon Country comes to lift your spirit, warm your heart, and renew your faith in the goodness of God who saw the first settlers through their strange and trying circumstances. **Diary of A Loving Heart**, a sequel to **Love is a Gentle Stranger** and **Love's Silent Song**, is a continuing saga of two vibrant and independent girls who came West to escape their pasts and seek new adventures. In their new home, they found the love of two fine men, a host of caring friends, and renewed their acquaintance with a caring God. But they found tragedy and conflict as well . . . until, in miraculous ways, they were able to resolve their problems and win against impossible odds. Those ways will surprise you!

Diary of a Loving Heart promises readers a new kind of courage, a new appreciation of beauty that celebrates life. With its reading, may you find a new appreciation of all that is lovely and a gentle reminder that the Almighty looks after His children!

June Masters Bacher

CONTENTS

CAST OF CHARACTERS

Chris Beth (Christen Elizabeth Kelly Craig, wife of minister)

Joe ("Brother Joseph," Joseph Craig, minister)

Vangie (Mary Evangeline Stein North, wife of doctor, Chris Beth's half sister)

Wilson ("Uncle Wil" North, doctor)

Young Wil (Wilson's nephew)

Marty (Martin, adopted son of the Craigs)

"True" North (Trumary North, daughter of Norths— Wilson's stepdaughter)

"Miss Mollie" (Mrs. Malone, wife of the Irish O'Higgin)

O'Higgin (second husband of "Miss Mollie," stepfather of the six children belonging to her late husband)

Nate Goldsmith (self-appointed school board president and chairman of the board of deacons)

Abe and Bertie Solomon (proprietors of the general store)

Maggie Solomon (their daughter)

"Boston Buck" (Indian chief)

Alexander Oberon (new teacher from the East hired to "help" Chris Beth)

Pioneer spirit—hale and hardy—
Ever seeing needs of others:
Though pioneer fingers gnarl with hardship,
Pioneer hands are helpful hands.
When a cabin's freshly wind-chinked,
Floored with puncheons, roofed with sky;
Ere the night falls, earnest effort
Will shingle out that patch of blue.
Coming with their bulging baskets,
Faces glowing in the hurry
Of the greetings and the work,
Happy children clapping, singing,
"London Bridge is Falling Down,"
Breezes blowing, wafting echoes
Of the ringing nails above;
Women talking food and quilting;
Girls—their eager thoughts of love.
Crimson sunset fades to darkness,
Sleepy cricket tunes his fiddle;
"Step up, gents, and choose your partners,
Form a ring and circle left!"

1

"Tempus Fugit"

Mockingly, the grandfather clock chimed as Chris Beth closed the bedroom door with a silent turn of the knob and stepped into the hall. She had grown to dread the clock's mellow song since Vangie had fallen ill. There had been a time when the two of them laughed like the carefree sisters they were at the 24-note tune the bells rang out just before striking the hour.

"What does it play, Wilson?" Vangie had asked her husband.

"Tempus Fugit," he said.

Vangie's voice, as golden as her hair, rose an octave higher as always when she was excited. "Speak English, Wilson!" she had demanded, and then to Chris Beth, "He loves teasing me with Latin!"

"Time Flies." Even then, five years ago, Wilson's voice had been sober. Being a doctor made him more aware, she supposed. Of time. Of life. And death. Now the translation tore at her heart, too.

Deliberately, Chris Beth waited until the great clock tolled its inevitable stroke of twelve, before walking into the living room of the North home. Noon. And somehow the old clock knew. God had separated the darkness and light. But man had created an ingenious mechanism for marking equal periods of elapsing time and, in this case, housed the knowing instrument in a harmless-looking mahogany box.

Frightened, she walked toward the front window to look out at the August rain.

"*Tempus Fugit!*" The grandfather clock ticked on. *Oh, Vangie. . . Wilson. . . Joe!*

Vangie would sleep only a short while even with the aid of the pain killer. When she awakened, she would be asking for Wilson. He would need a meal beforehand, just as he had needed the few short hours away from the confines of Vangie's room, her suffering, and the inevitable feel of death. All else was secondary—even his practice.

Hurriedly, Chris Beth set to work cutting thick slices from a loaf of graham bread. As she buttered it she tried to remember which of the three men preferred mustard to green tomato relish on their ham sandwiches. But even as her mind, numbed with loss of sleep, tried to concentrate on so small a matter, Young Wil's "Whoa!" said that he, Wilson, and Joe were back from Turn-Around Inn and lunch was not nearly ready.

Today it had taken Vangie longer than usual to doze. The medication did less and less good. Vangie had asked for her diary then, but unable to find strength to write, wanted to talk. Then, finding no strength for talking either, she cried. The crying hurt worst of all. Chris Beth's heart broke anew with each tear that coursed down the Dresden-china features of her sister's fragile, but nonetheless beautiful, face. *Don't cry, Vangie. . . don't cry, darling. . . .* How many times had she, the older sister, whispered the words in their growing-up years? Vangie was afraid of storms. Vangie was afraid of the dark. Vangie was afraid of the wind. . . mice in the attic. . . the bears beneath her bed! Only this time, there was no way Chris Beth could bring reassurance. Death, the Grim Reaper, would not go away.

Busying her hands helped, Chris found. Purposefully, she set about peeling the last of the fall tomatoes. There would be no time for the fried potatoes Wilson, his always-hungry nephew, and her husband enjoyed. But coffee, strong coffee. They would need that.

"Horses are curried." How good to hear Young Wil's everyday comment. Chris Beth turned from the woodstove to look at the lanky youth. How like Wilson he looked, more like son than nephew—same dark eyes, broad shoulders, teasing manner. What concerned her was the 14-year-old's temperament, such a private person and yet so hard-loving. *What*, she asked herself as she asked God in her prayers over and over, *are these two men I love so much going to do without the woman they are going to lose? And what can Joe and I do to ease the pain?* Joe being a minister would help but—

Chris Beth was unaware that Young Wil had crossed the kitchen until he interrupted her thoughts with a wave of his hand in front of her eyes. "Yoo-hoo!"

"Sorry," she mumbled and moved into action again. "Want to set the table for me?"

"Anything to speed up production." Then, after a clatter of dishes, he asked, "How is she?"

Chris Beth concentrated on measuring coffee into the pot before asking softly, "Can't you bring yourself to call Vangie—well, something other than *she*?"

"Like what?" She didn't need to look up to know that the brown eyes had turned sullen and defiant.

"Try *Mother*. It would make her so happy—Aunt Vangie—even Vangie—"

"She's not my mother—or my real aunt—just my uncle's wife."

"I know, darling. But I am only your teacher, and the two of us have such a good understanding. I just wish—"

"*I* just wish *you'd* have married Uncle Wil!"

Chris Beth stared at him, stunned. She felt confused, her heart pumping wildly in her chest. Abruptly, he turned and stalked away.

When the boy mumbled something inaudible at the door, Chris Beth turned in hope of hearing his words. But to her amazement, Joe and Wilson were standing silently, watching the retreating figure. *How long had they been at the door? How much had they heard?*

"Oh, I didn't see you," she said too quickly. "Oh, the coffee!"

It was too late. The pot had boiled over. She grabbed at the handle, burning her fingers.

"Here, let me." Wilson took the sticky pot from her hand,

poured out three cups, and set the granite vessel on the edge of the stove.

The brown liquid hissed on the hot stove, rolled into steaming droplets, and disappeared. But the odor of parched coffee filled the room. "I'm sorry," she murmured.

"No problem an open window can't handle," Joe said in the gentle manner she had come to expect of her husband. It won her heart and his congregation.

Returning to where Chris Beth stood, he smoothed the dark tendrils of her hair from her forehead and kissed her. "You are overtired, Chrissy. You must get some rest. You'll be needed even more later."

Joe's gentle words and the concerned look in his hazel eyes brought a semblance of order to her world. *I wish,* she thought fleetingly, *we were alone. . . that Joe would take me in his arms. . . that we were back to the way things used to be. I wish, oh! I wish, time did not fly. . . .*

But before the thought was so much as completed, the great clock chimed with warning and there was a small moan from Vangie's bedroom.

2

A Matter of Time

Monday!

Only a week remained before Chris Beth would be returning to her teaching position. Vangie's illness had left no time for preparing her clothes, sorting through books, or talking with school board members about the possibility of adding another teacher. With all the newcomers, school enrollment had mushroomed. But clothes, books, and enrollment were not the main concern. Vangie had always kept Marty....

"What," Chris Beth asked Joe over and over, "am I to do about the babies?"

And each time Joe laughed softly at her question. "They're hardly that any more—babies, that is."

Well, no. Hard as it was to believe, their Marty and Vangie and Wilson's Trumary were five years old. Marty had long since rebelled at their pet name of "Little Mart." With a jutting out of his round chin, which revealed the endearing dimple more than he knew, he declared himself a "big boy." The gesture hurt. He was growing too fast. And time was slipping away—without any more children. More than anything Chris Beth longed to bear Joe a child. But he has a son, Mrs. Malone said. *No, a son of his very own—his "own seed," wasn't that what the Bible said?* Humph! Brother Joe wasn't carin' none that his son was *grafted* onto the family tree. You Craigs love Little Mart much as the parents he

15

lost in the flood. *Oh, that was true*, Chris Beth hastily agreed. *Still*, she wondered, *why should Abraham's wife pray for a son and God hear her prayers and not hear mine?*

"Not to worry!" the older woman assured her wisely. "Just you wait'll you get to be Sarah's age!"

Chris Beth never talked about her barren condition with Joe. He was so protective. So dear. So gentle. Joe was the kind of husband who would feel the fault was within himself if he sensed that Chris Beth were unhappy. Of course, she and Vangie talked, but their conversations centered on Vangie's despair, not her own. It seemed so unfair, Vangie lashed out, when her only pregnancy by Wilson ended in miscarriage. Life was unfair. Wilson was unfair for refusing to allow her to take the risk of another pregnancy. Maybe even God was unfair! So Chris Beth found herself reassuring her younger sister as her dear friend Mollie Malone had reassured her. "Wait until we're as old as Sarah!" Only Vangie wasn't amused. That would be too late, Vangie said sadly with a sort of premonition in her usually tinkling voice.

And how right she was. Even as the original pain of her loss lessened, Vangie lamented the fact that Wilson was being denied a man's "natural pride" in having a child of his "own flesh and blood." Then, realizing what she had said, Vangie clapped her hand over her mouth as she did in her childhood when she had said something wrong. "Forgive me, Chrissy! At least, True is of *my* own body—oh, what *am* I saying? Those words must make you feel worse."

Yes, considering the circumstances. But neither husband seemed to care a fig! Wilson adored his fairy-princess daughter and seemed to give no thought to her not being his own "flesh and blood." And, of course, Joe idolized the orphaned Marty, his "frog prince."

Maybe, Chris Beth found herself thinking, *it's better this way. There are going to be so many things we have to decide even now. And more children would only compound the problem for us all. . . .*

"You weren't going to cry today. You weren't going to *think*. Rest, that's what Wilson sent you home for," Joe said unexpectedly from the door.

Chris Beth walked gratefully into her husband's arms. "I know," she sobbed. "I know. It's just the sight of our cabin...the memories...."

Joe wiped a tear from the tip of her nose. "...And worrying about the future?"

At her nod, he ushered her toward the kitchen. "You're to sit down and look out the window. See? It's stopped raining. I'll heat you some bath water, take Marty with me and—"

I'll get in the tub for one mighty long bath. Some soap would be nice—the kind with heliotrope in it like the last batch I made for Vangie and myself. She would nap briefly for the very first time in months. Then maybe, just maybe, Marty would rest...and she and Joe could steal a few precious moments all to themselves...he would hold her tight, kiss her lightly, then harder....

Between the line-dried, lavender-scented sheets, Chris Beth drifted into what should have been a blissful sleep. Instead, she dreamed wildly that she, Joe, Vangie, and Wilson were trying to synchronize their clocks. Through a dark layer of slumber, she heard Joe call across the creek to announce the time by the tiny, hand-carved cuckoo clock above their kitchen table. She ran into the bedroom to set the alarm clock at his count of, "One, two, three!" But, even as the cuckoo clock hiccuped the time, there came the mellow chime of the huge grandfather clock in the Norths' Big House playing its haunting 24-note tune ahead of the cabin clocks. Frantically, the two of them ran back and forth, adjusting the hand backward and forward—all the while knowing that the pendulum of the grandfather clock was swinging faster...faster...*faster!*

With a little cry, she awoke. Someone had rapped sharply at the door.

3

Like the Fragment of a Dream

Young Wil, white-faced and breathless from running, talked rapidly. "*Come*...come with me...please. *She*—I mean Vangie's worse—"

If the boy said more, Chris Beth failed to hear. With the kind of automatic responses born of fear, she dressed, followed Young Wil across the footlog, and entered the back door of the great, white farmhouse. Wilson, looking haggard and older than a man under thirty should, left Vangie's bedroom to meet them in the hall.

"I'm so tired," he said, swaying slightly on his feet. The way his hand crossed his face tore at Chris Beth's heart. The gesture meant to convey fatigue. But it conveyed more. The sensitive hand that had delivered babies, set limbs, and done delicate surgery, when more practiced physicians might have given up, conveyed grief—the kind of grief a strong man feels and dares not show.

I'm grieving with you, her heart cried out. *And yet neither of us can let go and comfort each other the way we should. We're afraid we will fall apart completely...be found out by others...or, worse, by ourselves. Must we always be so stoical because others think we are brave?*

But, with professional control, Wilson straightened. "Did you get any rest?"

"A little," Chris Beth said. "Enough to talk with Vangie if that's what she wants—and you think it's all right."

"Go on in. She wants to talk—alone," Wilson looked at Young Wil meaningfully. A look of relief passed over the boy's face. He hurried out the back door leaving Chris Beth and Wilson alone.

For just a moment neither of them moved. It would be hard, Chris Beth thought in some far-off corner of her mind, to describe the minuteness of that moment. In a sense, it seemed even less than the second between the *tick*-to-*tock* of the grandfather clock in its shadowy corner. But, in a greater sense, that moment's time was an eternity when soul and body were one.

How did it happen? When did it begin—or end? Or did it happen at all? Could it be the fragment of some dream that neither of them could remember? The mind could not be trusted and neither could the heart when the body was so fatigued, the emotions so drained, and grief—so long denied—swept down all defenses.

Wilson must have moved toward her, for when his arms reached out she walked into them—without seeming to walk at all. Like a puppet on a string. With no will of her own. No voice. No feelings. And there they were—two heartbroken figures drawn together and suspended by the magnet of grief they were powerless to control, unable even to put feelings into words that might have helped.

Then, just as quickly as her brother-in-law had embraced, he let her go. The *tock* of the second had ended, but Chris Beth knew that she had caught a rare glimpse of Wilson. He needed comfort and reassurance just as much as the patients who came to him. The sad difference was that Wilson refused all balm, ointments, and poultices of concern. And nobody—except for herself in this rare moment—realized that man and doctor were at points very far apart.

The clock ticked on as Wilson commented, "A pendulum's the most restless thing in the world. It no sooner gets to one side than it turns around and goes the other."

Chris Beth nodded mutely. *And all the springs, sprockets, weights, and chains reassemble themselves. Time flies. And life goes on. . . .*

"Try to get some rest, Wilson." With that, she turned and walked into her sister's room.

4

"It Is Finished!"

Vangie's golden hair lay spread out like an open fan on the rumpled lace-edged pillow slip. The flawless skin, which yesterday had looked like exquisite, blue-veined marble, no longer looked white. There was a tinge of yellow in the pallor today. And the kind of frightening serenity that said her suffering had ended. There was no movement except for one lone tear which had escaped the closed eyelids and slid slowly downward. *In the same way,* Chris Beth thought sadly, *my darling sister is slipping to the end.*

Sensing her presence, Vangie whispered weakly, "Don't let me be afraid, Chrissy."

Chris Beth knelt beside the bed and took the cold fingers in her hands. "There's no need to be frightened, darling."

It was true. Vangie had given her heart to the Lord long ago. A fierce, frightened child—victim of a "hell-fire and damnation" father—she had learned to love God in a new way here in the Oregon Country. How often she had said, "I'm not afraid of dying, Chrissy. It's *death* I hate!"

"Remember how I used to be so afraid—" Vangie paused to cough but resumed talking when the spasm passed. "—so afraid of everything? Thunder, the devil, bad dreams—and *him?*"

Vangie's father. Chris Beth's stepfather. "I remember, Vangie." Chris Beth tried to keep her voice unemotional. "But you're not afraid now—"

The wide, violet eyes opened. "Except that there won't be time to talk."

"There will be time," Chris Beth said with a certainty she did not feel. Then, massaging the almost transparent fingers as if to sustain life, she added soothingly, "Just 'begin at the beginning and stop at the end,' like in *Alice in Wonderland.*"

There was a flicker of a smile. "I was scared of childbirth, too."

"But you made it!"

"*We* made it—you, Wilson, and I. Remember?"

Chris Beth forced a small laugh. "I'm not likely to forget."

Vangie seemed to breathe for the first time. "That makes True part yours, Chrissy—you'll look after her—you and Wilson?"

"How could you ask, Vangie? True's a part of us all—and a part of Joe as well. Let's talk about what's troubling you."

It was important that Vangie conserve her energy. And, yes, it seemed important, too, that the conversation turn to something which had no connection with the circumstances of True's birth. This was no time to remember the painful past. She had long since forgiven her younger sister's folly. It no longer hurt that Vangie's precious little daughter belonged to Jonathan Blake, Chris Beth's one-time fiance.

"Vangie?" she prompted when the silence became prolonged.

Vangie opened her mouth to speak and was seized by another spasm of coughing. Each cough was like a knife in Chris Beth's heart.

"Some day—some day there will be a way to conquer this disease," Chris Beth whispered, as she tried to control the coughing by shielding her sister's fragile body with her own. "Wilson has promised!"

When Vangie spoke again, her voice was weaker. What she had to say must be said quickly. Panicky, Chris fought between calling Wilson and waiting to hear what Vangie needed to say privately.

Seeming to sense the thought, Vangie gripped Chris Beth's hands with all her strength. The grasp was like that of a baby bird which, knowing it is futile, clutches at the straw of a wind-rocked nest.

"*Stay*—I need you—not them—" she gasped.

There was no decision to make. Vangie's needs came first. "Relax, darling. I am here."

"It is finished!"

Vangie closed her eyes. Chris Beth waited. The fragile form under the light cover seemed motionless. But there was more to say! *Dear God, not yet. . . .*

"Vangie!"

"It is finished—the diary." The words were no more than a whisper.

Chris Beth inhaled gratefully. "Is *that* all?" She managed a light laugh which sounded as forced as it was.

The younger girl tried to lift her head then fell back weakly. "Is that *all*? Chrissy—it's everything—it's for you— you alone. . . read. . . do it. . . *for me. . . .*"

The weak breathing became labored. When Chris Beth asked if she should send for the others, there was no reply. Dropping the limp hands quickly, she fled in search of Wilson.

Vangie's words were forgotten in the wave of grief that spread over her. Overcome by near-hysteria, Chris Beth was unable to see the tall figure at the door. When strong hands grasped her arms, making her a prisoner, she tried to wrench away.

"Wilson! I have to find Wilson!"

"Get hold of yourself, Chris Beth!" Wilson's voice. Wilson's strong hands. But not Wilson the man. . . Vangie's husband. . . the best friend of her husband. Wilson the *doctor*!

As professionally as if he were calming a distraught child who feared an iodine swab on a small cut, Wilson said, "You will be all right."

How dare he talk down to her! How *could* she have been attracted to this heartless, arrogant, domineering man before she met Joe—before Vangie followed her out West? Wildly, she searched for words that could wound as she was wounded. Her grief *must* find expression.

"I'll hate you all my life for this!"

"Probably," he said, dropping his hands from her arms

and hurrying into Vangie's room. But Chris Beth was too buried in her suffering to catch the pain in his voice.

Slowly, the world righted itself. Somewhere a rooster crowed. That meant "company coming," Mrs. Malone said. And high above her own little world there was the unmistakable frost-remembered cry of wild geese. Canadian honkers seeking warmer climes. That meant winter. Then, from closer at hand, there came the carefree tinkle of childish laughter. Never mind the "signs" or the seasons. Life went on forever, like the creek the children loved, or the river that hugged the valley.

With a calm that surprised her, Chris Beth joined Wilson at Vangie's bedside. Wilson looked up. His face was stricken. But there was welcome in his brown eyes. The moment in the hall, like the one preceding it, would never be forgotten—completely—by either of them. But both encounters would be stored away, never to be shared, never to be reviewed or even understood. Raw emotions. Revealing. But past.

"She's gone, Chrissy."

"I know," Chris Beth said.

And then the others were all there. Later, she was to remember that Joe's arm was around her shoulder, that Marty clung tightly to her hand, and that Young Wil, with tears streaming down his face unchecked, went quietly to stand beside his uncle.

Wilson scooped True up and let her look directly into her mother's face. Like a tintype picture the family stood there, the silence unbroken.

"Does my mommy hurt worse, Daddy?" True whispered at last.

Wilson smoothed back the golden curls and kissed the tiny Vangie-in-miniature. "Not now, darling," he said softly. "Not ever again."

"Is she up in heaven with God?"

"She's there—or on her way." Chris Beth heard the catch in Wilson's voice and regretted with all her heart the harsh words she had spoken in her helplessness and pain.

"Did you see the angels, Daddy, when they came for Mommy?"

There was silence. *Why, he can't answer*, Chris Beth realized suddenly. *Not that he is unable to find the words but that he cannot find the voice.*

She knew the words, too. But dare she try to speak? The next moment would leave a lasting impression with the small children. She looked pleadingly at Joe, but he seemed unable to respond. But, of course! Her husband's slight stammer would return as always during stress. True's great violet eyes were on Wilson's face. And Chris Beth realized that Marty clung even harder to her hand. A slight whimper would open the floodgates. *Oh, dear God, for strength!*

"Very few people ever see angels, I guess. But I'll bet your daddy and Aunt Chrissy felt them hovering close." Young Wil spoke loudly and clearly.

"That we did, darling," Chris Beth agreed, finding her asked-for strength. "That we did."

She turned away then, no longer able to keep her strange emotions tethered. The months of her sister's illness had stratified her feelings, layering the first concern with shock, then overlaying the combination with pain, fatigue, and fear. Later came confusion, hysteria, bitterness, and anger, followed by today's sorrow which solidified all layers. And yet, it was Young Wil who found the strength for the greatest hour of need—a strength, which like the river, would sustain them all. Chris Beth felt pride, then a sad-sweet bud of acceptance.

"We will pray now," Joe said without the hint of a slur in his speech. Silently, he knelt beside the bed. The others, as was their custom, joined hands and waited for his words.

"Lord," Joe spoke softly but audibly above the chiming of the great hall clock tolling out the fourth hour that memorable August afternoon. "Lord, there is no need to explain our pain to You. Each time we lose a loved one, we get a better idea of what it was like for You to lose Your Son. But we praise You for the hope that sacrifice cost. And we ask that, through that hope, our pain will ease. Keep Vangie close in spirit—living, laughing, and moving among us—until we are reunited. Don't let us lose our way! Amen."

Joe rose and placed a hand to Chris Beth's elbow, ushering her quietly out of the room. Marty hung back, wanting to remain with True, his constant companion. But Young Wil, who was following the Craigs, leaned down to take the small hand.

"We have lots of work to do, fellow! How would you like to ride over to Turn-Around Inn—and maybe into Centerville?"

Marty's eyes lit up and his mouth made a perfect "O." The older boy was barely able to close a silencing hand over the pursed lips in time to stop the squeal of glee. A horseback ride...a peppermint...life went on....

Chris Beth hurried toward the stove. Neighbors would be coming. They would need coffee. And she needed the activity. Wilson would not prolong True's good-bye to her mother. Joe would help him then with what needed doing before the others came. *Don't think...move...hurry....*

"Are you all right, honey?" Chris Beth jumped at the sudden sound. She had gone into action automatically as it seemed she had been compelled to do all her life. In that reflex, she had actually forgotten the existence of her husband and son.

"I'm fine—really, I am—oh, Joe! I appreciate you so much."

"And I appreciate you, God knows!" The words, torn from him, were almost a groan. "I was thinking in there—I—I don't know what I would do—"

When Joe stopped, Chris Beth supplied the words because they were hers, too. "Without me? I know. I feel the same."

Was it strange that the two of them should embrace in the house so recently visited by death's angel? Chris Beth did not find it so. She was feeling a kind of numbness. The pain would return and have to be dealt with. But for now, her great loss had served to remind her what a precious gift from God life was. Vangie had learned that through her suffering. That undoubtedly accounted for the painfully-scribbled diary she insisted be propped up in bed to write in until the last. Chris Beth would look for it—in time...but for now, she must leave her husband's loving arms and be ready for the hours ahead. She pulled away regretfully.

Chris Beth removed the pound cake from the cupboard.

Still nice and moist. *Better,* she thought, *than any store-bought cake at the bakeries back home.* She sliced it, then remembered that she probably looked a mess. She and Vangie always made a point of "staying beautiful here on the frontier," as Vangie had phrased it. Certainly, today was to be no exception. Vangie would want all their practices to go on.

Laying down the knife, Chris Beth crossed the kitchen to look at herself in the mirror above the sideboard. But she was unable to see in the gathering darkness. Best light the lamps... *keep busy, keep busy...* and brush her hair.

The reflection she saw, in the glow of lamplight, was reassuring. Her dark, straight-browed countenance was no match for Vangie's golden fragility. But it stood up better under stress. There were no purple shadows to reveal her loss of sleep. Even her heavily-fringed eyelids carried no hint of pink to tell the world how many tears she had shed. *Brush, brush, brush... one hundred strokes makes the hair glossy. Braid, swirl upward, secure with a comb—maybe letting a tendril or so escape—*

Chris Beth was suddenly aware of a tug on her long skirt. It was such a gentle tug that she wondered how long it had gone unnoticed.

"Oh, True—darling," she murmured leaning down to kiss her fair-haired niece. "Aunt Chrissy didn't know you were here."

"I didn't want you to know. I just wanted to watch. Your hair's so *be-U-tiful!* Why do you and Mommy look different?"

"Well, for one thing, we have different fathers," Chris Beth answered, being careful to use present tense as the child did.

True's golden head bobbed in understanding. "Like me and Marty."

"Sort of, yes."

True seemed about to say something then changed her mind. Instead, she drew a long, shuddering breath. Surely she would break into tears and that would be better. Wouldn't it? But there were no tears, just words.

"Do you want me to set the table? Mommy lets me help."

Chris Beth was uncertain whether to be relieved or disappointed. Maybe if they could have cried together...but she would go along with whatever True wanted. They would feel their way together.

"I *do* need help. There will be lots of people—coming for the wake. Do you know what a wake is?" Chris Beth asked gently.

Again the bobbing of the little head. "Daddy told me. It's lots of friends. To keep Mommy company. He's gonna let me light the candles. Are these the right cups, Aunt Chrissy?"

Holding back the tears, Chris Beth set out as many cups as she was able to find. Joe would need to add hers to the number as soon as he found time to make a trip to the cabin.

"Marty will be back soon—he's gone to tell the others—to ask them to come—" Chris Beth found herself stumbling for words for the first time with True. Wise for her age, the child would suspect. "You and he can play then, like always," she tried to sound more natural.

"No," True said soberly. "I can help you get Mommy ready. Daddy told me I could."

Something akin to anger flared in Chris Beth again. *How dare Wilson expose a five-year-old to this! Oh, there are so many things to be set straight! But this is not the time. I must think of True only.*

Outside, the air turned chill. Early autumn mists turned to a drizzle and Chris Beth was grateful to see that Joe had laid the first fire of the season in the fireplace.

"Shall we light it now, True?" she asked, noting that the child's tiny face was pressed against the window, the little button nose flattened comically against the cold pane.

True blew her breath against the glass and wiped it away with her right forefinger. "You light it. I'm watching."

Watching for Young Wil and Marty, most likely. And they should be back. She stooped to light the fire, then watched in momentary fascination as the hot blue flames cooled to yellow. *If only this were a normal evening—*

Resolutely, she put aside the thought. There was work to be done, she reminded herself firmly. First, though, she had to try to unveil little True's thoughts...break down the barriers...become a new family....

"Come and warm your hands, honey," she coaxed. "The fire's so pretty. One of these nights soon we'll pop corn—"

True's finger traced a wide, wet circle on the glass before she answered. "It won't be the same."

"No," Chris Beth said slowly, wondering what more to say. One did not deal with this child with vague words intended to divert her attention. Like Vangie in appearance, True was more like Chris Beth in her behavioral patterns. They thought alike and hurt alike, but there was a toughness of moral fiber inside them that demanded the truth.

Suddenly, True's hand dropped to her side. Her back went rigid as she strained forward to peer into the darkness. "They're here," she whispered. "Oh, Aunt Chrissy, they've come back!"

Chris Beth hurried to the window. The snort of a horse sent a wave of relief over her being.

"Sure enough, they have!" she said with a little cry of joy. "Oh, how good to have Marty and Young Wil home safely. Let's go meet them."

She reached to take True's hand, but the child drew back. The great blue eyes were purple by the glow of the firelight—purple and filled with despair. An enormous tear rolled down the doll-like face.

"I wasn't waiting for *them*. I—I'm watching for the angels—to bring my mommy back!"

"Oh, my darling," Chris Beth said softly, kneeling down beside the tiny figure. "I know you're hurting. I know—because I hurt, too!"

"I don't hurt! I—I—" But the defiant little words were drowned out by convulsive sobs. "Oh, Aunt Chrissy—"

Chris Beth gathered her close. "Cry, darling. It's all right to cry—we'll cry together!"

5

The "Second Day" Dress

Neighbors came, bringing food and consolation. Chris Beth went through with it all in a white haze, aware of subdued voices, busy hands, and the sound of her own voice asking questions, answering them, even giving directions at times, yet knowing all the while that she was lying in the lap of a great pain—so great that it would blot out all detailed memory.

Faces she loved floated in and out....Joe, gentle and caring...Wilson, solemn and withdrawn...Young Wil, youthfully masterful...True, watchful, waiting...Marty, uncertain...and the countless settlers, supporting and loving, at their best in time of crisis.

Only a few incidents stood out before the funeral—Mrs. Malone's arrival, the "second day" dress, and little True's "getting Mommy ready."

Mollie O'Higgin Malone, the beloved friend who had taken her in as a stranger and welcomed Vangie—accepting her out-of-wedlock "condition" when others whispered unthinkable words—was her usual no-nonsense, efficient self.

"Let the horses browse, O'Higgin," Mrs. Malone said to her husband. "I declare that Irishman gets more helpless with ev'ry passin' day!" she added good-naturedly, embracing Chris Beth as she spoke.

Chris Beth felt herself smile through her tears. It was good to be drawn close to the broad bosom, to be loved and treated ever so briefly like a child herself, and to inhale the "gingerbread sweetness" of Mrs. Malone, who had mothered her from the moment they met.

But the older woman did not prolong the greeting. "Now then," she said with practicality, "the men'll take care of the grave and all. Let's us women get Vangie ready."

True's little ears, from wherever she was standing, picked up the words. "I'm going to help," she said, drawing herself up to her full five-year-old height as soon as she stood beside Chris Beth.

"Well, let's see—" Mrs. Malone drummed on her chin with three fingers and hesitated, her faded eyes seeking Chris Beth's. At Chris Beth's nod, the older woman added, "I reckon as how there's a-plenty you can do."

"I reckon so," the child said solemnly.

Looking back on the situation, Chris Beth wondered later if she herself could have borne up as she did without the serenity of the older woman and the courage of the little child.

"I'll wash your face, Mommy," True whispered to Vangie, "but Aunt Chrissy'll do your hair. She knows how better 'cause she used to do it when you were little like me—"

As she worked gently, True kept humming a familiar tune. Chris Beth tried hard to identify it. Remembering seemed important.

"Brahms' 'Lullaby'!" she said aloud in sudden recognition.

Little True smiled then for the first time. "Mommy sings it to the bees. Remember?"

Present tense again! Chris Beth turned away to stem the flow of fresh tears. *Memories...bittersweet to me, the adult...but real, as yet, for her, the child.*

Even as she fussed with Vangie's flaxen tresses, fluffing soft curls about the temples and forehead the way she liked, Chris Beth found herself wondering: *How can I bring the two worlds together for her without letting them collide? How supportive will Wilson be in this—and, for that matter, with Young Wil? What's to become of him?*

Young Wil! Remembering his words, she stopped short: "I just wish *you'd* married Uncle Wil!" Ideas died hard with the boy.

True broke the silence in the room. "Are you stuck, Aunt Chrissy? It goes like this." And, taking the comb from Chris Beth's hand, she twisted a strand of her mother's hair around her small finger and pressed it close to the cheek— exactly where it should have been.

The two of them had been so engrossed that neither saw Mrs. Malone remove the top from a giant box and lay its contents at the foot of the bed. True, who was first to notice, gave a little gasp of delight.

"Oh, it's for Mommy, her right color, but—I wish she could've seen it—just once."

"She did, little darlin', she seen it just once. It was your mother's weddin' dress!"

Then, as they arranged the shimmering folds to cover the thinness of Vangie's wasted body, Mrs. Malone told True the beautiful story of the dress. It had belonged to herself, she said. 'Twas her "second day" dress, the custom of the time being that a bride must wear a new gown on the second day of her honeymoon. Vangie had borrowed it for her wedding trip. Why shouldn't she borrow it for this, the best trip of all? Wouldn't True agree? True would. Mrs. Malone told the whole story—except the part about the brooch. That part belonged to Chris Beth. Some day— maybe—it would belong to True also.

The story ended. Then, to the surprise of the two women, the golden head of the little child drooped wearily to her mother's bosom, nestling among the blue ruffles, where the flashing sapphire-and-pearl pin had nestled on her wedding day, and she slept.

The rest of the scenario, like that preceding it, went back into the white haze of Chris Beth's memory.

The black funeral carriage came from Centerville to bear Vangie's body to the newly staked out cemetery plot on the knoll east of the new church. There was rain—not heavy, just enough to gray the skies and dampen the dust so that it stuck to the wheels of the long line of wagons and buggies in the funeral procession.

For the first time, Chris Beth hated the rain. It seemed so wrong for a funeral, especially Vangie's. No, maybe it wasn't wrong at all. What kind of day would be right? Rain was too depressing. But sunshine would have been a mockery. . . .

Joe took complete charge of the service. Chris Beth marveled at his composure—not a hint of a stutter, not a quaver of the voice. She must tell Joe again, as she had so often in the past, what a comfort he was. And what a minister, husband, and father! It seemed only fitting that he should "stand up" with Wilson. After all, the two best friends had "stood up" together for the double wedding. Could there be such a thing as a "best man" at a funeral? she wondered foolishly through the colorless maze of her controlled grief.

Thoughtfully, the settlers turned away when the services ended, some going home and others returning to the North home to clear away any painful reminders and prepare the evening meal. Mrs. Malone and O'Higgin had to get back to Turn-Around Inn, thriving since dreams of the stagecoach link-up between California and Oregon had come to pass. But couldn't the "babies" go with them? Marty, always shy, clung to Chris Beth's skirt while True's violet eyes betrayed the feelings beneath the calm. *Any minute now,* the expressive eyes said, *the angels may come for another one of the people I love!*

"Another time," Chris Beth suggested significantly.

Mrs. Malone nodded with understanding. "But I'll be over. Meanwhile, keep a weather-eye cocked on Wilson. He's too tranquil-like."

"I don't know that I can do much for him, though," Chris Beth said.

Mrs. Malone turned to look directly into her face. "You're the only one who can."

When all had left but family, Wilson said to Joe, "Will you take the others home? I'd like to be left alone a little while."

Chris Beth hesitated, but Joe took her hand. "He must work his way through his grief. It will take time," he said softly.

When the children were in the buggy, Joe came to Chris Beth's side to help her step up. When she hesitated again, he said, "It's best this way. We must leave him, Chrissy."

Yes, it was best, she supposed, but she was unable to ride

away without looking back over her shoulder. What she saw hurt her worse than any of the months, weeks, days, and hours leading up to the single moment. Wilson—the laughing, carefree, teasing Wilson of old—stood alone. A solitary figure. . .beside the new mound. . . braced defensively against the chilling rain. . . .

"Turn away, Chrissy," Joe begged softly so that the children would not hear. "We have to look forward."

In a moment, yes, she would look forward. But it was too soon. There had to be some hope back there. Chris Beth, her heart breaking inside her, forced her tear-filled eyes to travel up from the sod to where the spire of the new church pointed heavenward. Then she turned to look forward with Joe.

Mellow light flowed from every downstairs window of the Big House. *I will take comfort in the small things,* Chris Beth thought, *and all they symbolize. . . .*

When Wilson came home, she longed to rush to meet him and offer words of comfort. But there was an invisible wall between them—one that neither of them seemed able to understand. The loss should have brought them closer together. Time. . .it would take time, Joe said.

"Can I get you anything—food—?" Meaningless words.

"Nothing, Chrissy." Wilson turned toward her, an unreadable expression in his weary face. "Just look after True—and excuse me to the others."

With that, he walked to the door of Vangie's bedroom. For a moment, she supposed he would enter. Instead, he pulled the door closed gently but firmly and, shoulders erect, walked up the curving stairs.

It had been a good marriage, approaching the ideal in Chris Beth's mind—almost, she sometimes thought, enviable. To Vangie, the dreamer, it had been a storybook romance. Just what it was to Wilson was difficult to tell. He hovered over Vangie, caring for her as one cares for a precious possession that breaks easily, but there was a part of Wilson he seldom revealed—a part unknown to light-hearted Vangie.

What*ever* the marriage was to him, it was over. Finished. Like Vangie's diary. . . .

6

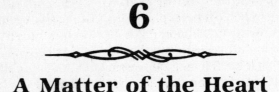

A Matter of the Heart

The funeral had occurred on Wednesday. On Thursday morning, long before dawn, Chris Beth sat at the kitchen table of the Big House alone, drinking coffee and making mental lists of all that must be done. Urgent. As soon as possible. And sometime. The "urgent" list meant school which was only four days away and topping it were the questions: *Who will care for Marty and True, and what about Young Wil who's ready for high school?*

Rain stomped against the roof. A branch from the giant fir tree scraped its thumbnails on an upstairs window. Chris Beth shivered and tried to shake off her depression. She had needed the privacy the early-rising promised, but she did not need the loneliness. And what was *that?* A whistle? At this time of day?

Sitting erect, she listened. The whistling grew more distinct, coming so close she was able to make out a tune. "My bonnie lies over the ocean," a great voice suddenly boomed.

O'Higgin! Chris Beth could imagine the crinkles of a smile around the merry blue eyes. Sometimes she wondered if everyone who lived in Ireland could be this cheerful and decided it was impossible.

Hurriedly, she unlocked the front door and, without lighting a lamp in the front room, motioned the ruddy-faced man into the kitchen.

"The others are sleeping," Chris Beth cautioned after a whispered greeting. Then, forcing a smile, she offered coffee.

"Sure'n 'twould be t'my likin', lass." The red-bearded face wreathed in a twinkling smile, O'Higgin removed his plaid jacket, shook off the droplets of rain, and sat down backward on a kitchen chair with his massive arms along the back of it. " 'Tis news I've brought—straught—?"

"*Straight,*" Chris Beth supplied as his "Mollie wife" would have done. She felt her depression turning to curiosity.

"Aye! Straight from hisself, the president of our board."

"Nate Goldsmith? But at this hour—?"

"Emergency meetin' it was. And the coffee, be it hot?"

Murmuring an apology, Chris Beth poured her self-described "gospel truth" friend a cup of his favorite brew. There could be no doubt about the meeting, but what could have been so important? Of course, one could expect anything in this strange, but wonderful, settlement!

Chris Beth concentrated on the little puddle of water made by O'Higgin's jacket he'd tossed carelessly on the floor. If Mrs. Malone were here—

Deliberately, O'Higgin stirred his coffee, sampled it, and let out an "Ah-h-h-h!" of satisfaction, before breaking the news. Circumstances of the morning forgotten, Chris Beth felt a stir of excitement.

"O'Higgin?" she prompted.

"Ah, yes, th' object of my call! Come Monday, ye be gettin' the help y'er needin' at school."

Chris Beth set her Spode cup down with a clatter. "You mean—you mean—" she said incredulously, "another *teacher?*"

"Th' same, lass. And now me Mollie Girl'll be wantin' a hand at the inn. 'Tis best I be goin' before we waken th' family."

"A little late, old-timer," Wilson spoke from the door.

The two men shook hands. There was no mention of Vangie's death or the funeral. Condolences were offered yesterday. And, while tears might be shed in secret, on the surface life in the valley went on.

" 'Twas news I brought," the Irishman said.

"I heard." No more and no less. Wilson helped O'Higgin with his jacket, shook his hand again, and sat down in the chair he vacated. Chris Beth followed their guest to the entrance, thanked him warmly, and closed the door behind his retreating figure before realizing she'd forgotten to ask if the new teacher would be a man or a woman.

Wilson had poured two cups of coffee when she returned to the table.

"Join me," he said quietly.

"I've had more than my ration," Chris Beth began. Then, seeing the glaze of sleeplessness in his eyes, she sat down knowing that he wanted to talk to her alone.

"What is it, Wilson?" she asked, hoping they could have a few quick exchange of words before the others came downstairs.

The tired brown eyes met hers with appreciation. "We have to decide about the future," he said simply.

Yes, heading her list was the future of the children. "Very true," she said slowly, stirring the coffee to which she'd forgotten to add sugar and cream. "I've been thinking about them—"

"Them? I mean *us*. Joe and me . . . you and me . . . the best of friends . . ."

Chris Beth felt a slow flush creep to her face. Her heart pumped against her ribs and it was difficult to breathe. The rain seemed to slow to a stop. Even the hiss of the black kettle softened to a sigh. The world was hushed around them. And for an impossible moment she and Wilson were back in the forest, young and carefree, crushing colored leaves beneath their feet . . . before they became family . . . .

Love was stronger than death. Vangie's absence couldn't erase that. Then, because she was frightened and surprised by her own doubts, her words came out harshly.

"*Friends?* Don't we mean more than that to you? We're a *family!*"

A look of surprise crossed Wilson's face, followed by hurt, then his eyes narrowed and he looked at her with something akin to mockery. At last he shook his head as if in disbelief.

"How is it that even under conditions like this," he

asked in a flat, emotionless voice, "you manage to misinterpret every word I say?"

"I—I—" Chris Beth began in hot denial. Then, ashamed and embarrassed, she spread her hands out in despair. Wilson was right. She had always read more into his words than was there.

Whatever his next words would be she deserved them. Averting her eyes, she waited.

"Your coffee's cold," he said suddenly. When she would have risen from the table, he pushed her down gently. Then, he walked to the side table, rinsed her cup in the basin of water, poured it full of coffee, and refilled his own cup.

Situation normal. Everything under control. He was back to the Wilson of old. Vangie might never have existed in his life. And she, Chris Beth, was reverting right back with him. Almost quarreling . . . and over what?

But when he spoke again, he was the Wilson of this day—a young doctor, bewildered widower, wondering how to pick up the pieces of his life.

"Will you and Joe move in with us?" he asked matter-of-factly, as if continuing a conversation.

Chris Beth measured sugar into a spoon, leveling it as if each grain counted. "I don't know," she answered, striving for his tone of voice. "I haven't talked it over with Joe."

"I talked it over with Vangie. She was going to write it all down for you—" His voice trailed off. Chris Beth waited for him to continue. Instead, he dropped his head into his hands with a slight moan.

Compassion washed over her. *Oh, Wilson! Forgive me,* her heart cried out. *I've let you down in your hour of need. . . let's start over. . . .*

Aloud she said, "It does seem practical. This is home to True and Young Wil. Home to Joe, Marty and me—and we all need each other—"

Wilson raised his head but did not meet her eyes. "Thank you, Chrissy," he said simply. "I'll make it as pleasant for you as I can. Even promise," he said, struggling for lightness, "not to bring in a new Ma!"

When Chris Beth gave a start, Wilson managed a little

laugh. "Just an idea of Nate's—presented at yesterday's service."

"Oh, Wilson! How thoughtless of him! Just overlook it. Mr. Goldsmith's very—well, insensitive—"

Wilson met her eyes then. "Don't let what he or anyone else says upset you, Chrissy. He means well. We will do as we see fit."

The hall clock struck six. Picking up the cups, Chris Beth hurried away from the table. "Better stoke the fire. I thought they'd all be up sooner," she said over her shoulder.

"Exhausted—like we are." Wilson opened the firebox of the big iron range and adjusted the draft. Pausing then, he said almost to himself, "Vangie says this beast is always hungry. There's a new kind, you know, on legs you can sweep under—has a warming closet, a water reservoir— she wants—*wanted*—" His voice broke.

"Oh, Wilson!" Chris Beth cried out, her voice breaking along with his, "Keep it like that. Keep it in the present. Keep Vangie with us."

Then, without reservation, she grasped both his hands in a natural gesture. He clung to them tightly, fighting for control. The fire in the grate crackled with warning and Wilson let go of her hands to close the damper of the stove. Then he turned back to her.

"You see how impervious I am to such suggestions as Nate's?"

"Of course, I do! It will take time for all of us."

"More than time, Chrissy," he said sadly. "Arrangements we can manage—you and Joe, the children—but marriage? Marriage is a matter of the heart."

7

Urgent, As Soon As Possible, And Sometime

Urgent! Maybe she'd said it aloud, Chris Beth thought in the half-light of Friday morning. She looked down at her husband, still bunched in sleep born of exhaustion, and tried to remember how much they'd been able to move from the cabin yesterday and what lay ahead today.

All in all, yesterday had gone well. Until the very last. *Maybe,* she thought, *moving possessions is easier than moving people.* There was very little left in the cabin—except a part of her heart.

Well, what had to be had to be. As quietly as possible, she eased out of bed, and—striving for her usual efficiency—began to dress for the new day. But, even as she hung the long nightgown on its peg, Chris Beth was aware of a musing frown. It all looked so easy. Just packing Joe's mother's china, rearranging it among Wilson and Vangie's...rolling up the bearskin rug...packing the family Bible, the research books, her school supplies. Nothing she, Joe, Wilson, and Young Wil (who was delighted) couldn't handle. *But how does one move a heart?* she had questioned at the last moment.

Seeming to sense her need, Joe had reached down from his great height and kissed her gently on the forehead. "Would you like to stay a minute after the rest of us go?"

39

With a lump in her throat, she had nodded. And there in the museum-quiet of the empty cabin, she cried out the sorrow in her heart. It wasn't as if the Big House were new. After all, the four of them had shared the warmth of its sturdy, wooden arms on all the firelit evenings they spent planning the double wedding. And during the past five years it had been a second home...but the cabin—the cabin was a *first*....

"Are you all right?" Joe asked out of the semi-darkness now.

Wonderful Joe! His voice came as no surprise. He always knew her moods. Even those, she was sure, that penetrated her sleep.

"I'm all right," she answered, realizing suddenly that she really was.

Marty, always adaptable, had taken the move in stride. Young Wil made no effort to hide his pleasure with the arrangements. And True's sober little face had softened with obvious relief at the news. So nothing remained but details the men could handle and adjusting which time would handle. "I'm fine," Chris Beth said with growing conviction.

"Good girl," Joe said, pulling himself up into a sitting position on the bed. "We can't always live by the old rules, can we?"

"No," Chris Beth said slowly. "We can't. So I guess we just have to invent new ones as life challenges us."

Joe set his feet experimentally on the floor. "It's safe," Chris Beth laughed, "but take this for good measure." She kicked the bearskin toward him and went into the side room to finish dressing.

Fumbling in the darkness of the small room, Chris Beth heard the scratch of a match and knew that Joe had lighted the kerosene lamp. She waited a moment and then called, "Are you decent yet?"

Even after five years of marriage, she was unable to resist teasing Joe a little. He was so serious, so earnest, so different from his lifelong friend. That is, the way Wilson was before Vangie's illness.

Joe never seemed to mind her teasing. Probably he was smiling. She could imagine him, his brown hair picking up bronze tones in the flood of lamplight. But Joe's voice sounded sober when he replied.

"Come on in. I need to know what new rules we're setting today."

Chris Beth crossed the room to sit down beside him on the bed. "No rules—just plans, priorities. There's so much to think about before Monday. Who can keep Marty and True now with—with Vangie gone?"

"Chrissy," Joe spoke slowly, "I've given this some thought and wondered—do you want to give up the idea of teaching this year?"

They had been all over this before. Joe should know they couldn't get by on what the church was able to pay, but how could she keep repeating the words without hurting him?

"I'm sure, Joe. I'm *very* sure. I love being with the children—and it's too late anyway. There's no time for finding another teacher."

Something clicked in her mind then. Her hand went to her throat with the sudden realization that she had forgotten to tell Joe about the new teacher!

"I can't believe this." The words were as much for herself as for her husband. "But somehow in all the turmoil of the past few days I didn't tell you about O'Higgin's news—"

"Wilson told me."

Did she imagine a touch of sadness in Joe's voice? No time to share with her husband. But time to share with another man? Nonsense! Joe knew better than that. Nevertheless, Chris Beth felt a need to reach up and pull his head to her shoulder. There had been so little *touching*—too little.

"I'm afraid I take you for granted, darling," she whispered.

Joe reached out with a suddenness that almost pushed her from the bed and drew her into such a tight embrace it was hard to breathe. "You just go on taking me for granted—always and always I'm yours!"

Joe's arms tightened, but Chris Beth pulled away. "Joe, the time! The children must be downstairs already—"

But the children were not downstairs! They were pounding on the door saying in one voice, " 'Open up! Or I'll huff and I'll puff and I'll blow your house down!' "

Joe grinned at Chris Beth, made an attempt at smoothing his hair, and opened the door. "Well, now," he said, "if it isn't 'The Three Little Pigs'!"

"Just two of 'em," Marty said excitedly. "Young Wil's with Uncle Wilson—and it's not about him, is it, True?"

"Not about him," True repeated soberly, but her eyes were dancing.

"Well then?" Chris Beth prompted.

True bit her bottom lip in mock concentration. Then, unable to hold back, she sang out, "Marty and I are going to start to school!"

Chris Beth felt her mouth fly open. Closing it quickly, she murmured, "We'll talk to Daddy about it, True."

"We talked it over already while you and Uncle Joe slept," she said.

"Then *Marty's* father has to think," Chris Beth said. "Five years old is awfully early—"

The two children, lined like twin soldiers, stared at her as if she had a lapse of memory. "We're smart," True said. "You said so!" Marty backed her up.

"Makes sense," Joe said slowly.

"Don't encourage this—yet," Chris Beth whispered to him. Then, smiling in spite of herself, she added, "You're as bad as they are!"

But, even as they all went downstairs together, Chris Beth knew that Item #1 on the "urgent" list had resolved itself. Item #2: Young Wil's education. Then today they must get to some of the "as soon as possible" items, going through Vangie's personal belongings, getting as much done as she could in advance of school's opening...oh, so much!

And some day, a long time from now, when the sharp pain of losing Vangie reduced itself to a dull ache, she would look for the diary. *But not now, Lord, not now. It would break my heart....*

8

Storm Warning

By Saturday, with everybody's help, the Big House took on a semblance of order. Chris Beth wondered if the others—especially Wilson—found as many painful reminders as she did. Vangie's clothes, always carelessly tossed, lay heaped in unexpected places. Then there was a lace-edged handkerchief waded into a little ball. She ironed it out with her hand the way Vangie did when deep in thought and the scent of violets was so real that Vangie might well have entered the room. Photographs of the beautiful, fragile face smiled hauntingly from bureau drawers. And, most painful of all to Chris Beth, was finding the jar of sweet-smelling ointment, lid screwed on but the contents deeply grooved where Vangie's slender, impatient fingers had dug out a pattern. Wilson shouldn't see this. It was too real. But smoothing the surface seemed cruel. Quickly, she screwed the lid back on and tucked the jar of ointment away.

A feathered fan Vangie had spread out grandly at her first ball...a memory book, the signatures now faded...Sunday school cards...and Mama's fur with tails. In a single day Vangie, darling Vangie's life passed in review. *It has to be—it has to be! If Wilson and True can hold up, so can I. If I crumple, so will they.* The unshed tears hurt so much more than those Chris Beth *had* shed. And yet, through it all, she clung to True's lovely widsom. Vangie would be with them forever...if they thought of her in present tense.

When Mrs. Malone came in the afternoon, Chris Beth gave her a running report. "We're moved in by mutual agreement, and we—all of us—are carrying on. I'm especially proud of True—no nightmares, crying, or anything that signals danger."

Mrs. Malone pushed at a stray lock of graying hair, tucking it neatly into the tightly-twisted knot on top of her head. "Like you—so like you—" she mused. "But 'twasn't True who had me worried. It's Wilson."

Chris Beth bit her lip. "He's fine—remarkably so."

The older woman was unconvinced. "*Too* fine. Not like 'im a-tall. Keep an eye on Wilson. Acceptance on his part's a storm warning!"

9

The New Schoolmaster

What is it that transforms this moment into a moment to remember? Chris Beth wondered as she watched little True standing silently beside Vangie's grave. *Silence!* That was it. The rains had stopped and on this bracing, blue-ribbon Sunday one could almost hear the silence of the dried grasses and the bulbs settling themselves down for the winter season ahead.

But as much as she hated the thought of breaking the lovely spell, Chris Beth knew by the warning of the church bell that it was time the two of them went inside. "We have to go, darling," she said softly, trying to avoid looking at the lettering on the white cross marking the mound of earth which already looked as if it belonged there.

True was not to be rushed. "What does it say, Aunt Chrissy? Does 'Vangie' begin with an E?"

"*Vangie* was a short way of saying *Evangeline*, True. Mary Evangeline North."

"Was Mommy's name always the same as Daddy's and mine?"

The question caught Chris Beth off guard. Certainly, it was not a subject that she wanted to go into now. One day, however, the matter would have to be dealt with. Right now, she would strive for a postponement.

"Your mother's name was once *Stein* just as yours is *North*. When you are married, you will have a new name, too."

45

True seemed satisfied, but something else troubled her. "Mommy's grave should have something on it—something pretty."

"It will in time," Chris Beth promised. "You and I will plant some violets for spring and chrysanthemums for autumn—"

"Mommy likes leaves better," True said. And before Chris Beth could restrain her, True ran to a nearby grove of vine maple and tugged at the lower branches until her small hands were filled with red-gold leaves.

Holding back tears, Chris Beth watched True scatter the leaves on the grave. Then, hand in hand, they walked quietly into the church. The singing was over and Joe had begun his message. Nobody would mind in this loving community where people helped in time of need but did not hover or condemn. How glad she was that this family could grow up in such a world—so different from the ritualistic services she and Vangie had been forced to endure in their childhood . . . where people had cared more about creeds and codes than faith.

Immediately after church Nate Goldsmith made his way to where Chris Beth stood in a group of women who had gathered to offer whatever help the family needed. It was obvious that the president of the school board was bursting with news.

Combing his sparse gray beard nervously with his right hand and gesturing with the other, Nate spoke confidentially. "He's here! Come to church the very first Sunday like'n the contract demands!"

Chris Beth knew, even before allowing her eyes to travel to the back of the big room where Nate pointed, that "he" referred to the new teacher. That she would be working with a man surprised and disappointed her. It would have been nice to have a woman, maybe somebody her own age. Not that a friend could replace Vangie, but—

"Seen 'im yet? The big feller with the strong right arm," Nate said with obvious pride.

It was easy to spot the newcomer, although *tall* would have been a more apt description than *big*. Some six feet eight or nine inches, a young man with incredibly blonde hair towered above the other men around him. *Strong arms? Maybe. They were certainly long enough, to make him look comically like Ichabod Crane.*

Repressing a smile, Chris Beth said, "I can't tell you how pleased I am that I will be having a helper."

Nate's pale eyes opened wide in surprise. "I'm obliged to tell yuh it's gonna be t'other ways around! It's only natural his bein' a man'n all that I've elevated Mr. Oberon to principal. So y'll be takin' orders from him."

Chris Beth drew herself up with a straightness matching the board member's. "He and I will have a lot to learn from each other," she said stiffly. "But as for my taking *orders*," she paused to suck her breath in, "that remains to be seen."

At that exact moment, the new teacher, who had been elbowing his way forward, paused beside Nate Goldsmith and extended a hand. Vigorously, it pumped Nate's smaller one and then dropped to dangle several inches below the sleeve of his shadow-check doublet-style jacket. But not before Chris Beth caught, with each pump, a glimpse of his bright-red waistcoat beneath the jacket. Had anybody dressed like that since the Renaissance? Surely no man in his right mind would wear such clothes to school!

Nate turned to Chris Beth. "Mr. Alexander Oberon!" he said with the pomp usually reserved for a formal ball.

"How do you do—and welcome, Mr. Oberon," Chris Beth said as warmly as she was able. "I'm Chris—"and then, unable to resist using the same formality Nate had used, "I'm Christen Elizabeth Craig."

Alexander Oberon accepted her outstretched hand and pumped it as vigorously as he had pumped Nate's. "My pleasure, Miss Craig—"

"*Mrs.* Craig," Chris Beth corrected quickly.

With obvious disappointment in his pale blue eyes, the new teacher murmured an apology. But he continued to hold her hand.

Withdrawing it as unobtrusively as possible, Chris Beth wondered if she should straighten her tucked-velvet turban. The hat was six years old now and the wire frame bent easily. Surely her head had bobbed up and down during the handshake!

Regaining her dignity, she said politely, "You had no way of knowing. I am—"

But Nate interrupted. "Chris Beth here's the wife of Brother Joseph."

"I see," Mr. Oberon fingered his beaver derby. "Well, I look forward to a good year. I can foresee a lot of changes."

So can I, Chris Beth thought inwardly. Striving for a natural voice, she answered, "It should be a successful year. We're all so thankful for the larger school—the new books—"

Alexander Oberon didn't seem to hear. "I have a lot of new ideas from the *East.*" The way he emphasized the word sounded as if nobody west of the Mississippi had heard it before. "But I sense in you, Miss—Mrs.—Craig, a person of Eastern *bel esprit.*"

Chris Beth felt her face flush as the puzzling young man bowed and made his way toward the front door of the church.

When he was out of hearing distance, Nate turned to her in bewilderment. "What on earth was he talkin' about—the bell-*what?*"

"*Bel esprit?*" She smiled. "It looks even worse written down—meaning having wit and a fine mind—French, I think."

Nate shook his head doubtfully. "Well, I'll be sprinkled! Am I gonna haf to get the ole woman of mine to interpret ever' word fer 'im? Who'd a'thought havin' a French-German wife a blessin'?"

From the corner of her eye Chris Beth saw Brother Amos and the other "disciples" gathering their families to leave the worship service. Excusing herself from Nate, she hurried to greet them. It was so good to have the Shaker group join in with them here. But even as she spoke briefly with the rather retiring women, her mind kept going back to the new schoolmaster.

It should be an interesting year—maybe amusing at times. But, as much as she welcomed another teacher in the school, Chris Beth felt a strange foreboding. Did it have to do with school? She wasn't sure.

10

Unexpected Decision

On Monday morning Chris Beth was awakened by a clatter of pots and pans, sounds she thought at first were a part of her dream. At the cusp of dawn, she tried to remember why this day was special even as she strained her ears to identify the sounds from somewhere below. But thinking was hard after working until midnight putting together— *what was it? Oh, yes! School supplies!* She'd overslept on the first day!

Automatically, she reached for Joe, then finding his side of the bed vacant and not even warm, she hurriedly backed out of bed wishing hard for unstuck eyes, her toothbrush, and a cup of coffee. As if some good fairy had heard her wishes, they were—in part—granted. She couldn't be dreaming the smell of coffee! Neither, she decided, slipping into the ruffled white blouse and long black skirt carefully laid out the night before, did she imagine the voices of Marty and True below.

"Tomorrow," Chris Beth had overheard True telling Marty last night, "will be the most *extreee*-ordinary day we ever lived!"

"*Extree*-ordinary," Marty mouthed. If True said so, it was true.

Probably neither of them slept a wink, Chris Beth thought, as with practiced hands she brushed, braided, and secured her heavy hair in a halo style. No time to button high-top shoes. Bedroom shoes for now.

Downstairs, to her surprise, breakfast was almost ready. Young Wil, fortunately, had supervised. He smiled a greeting, but the younger children hardly looked up.

"They're packing their lunch," Young Wil smiled.

Chris Beth squeezed his hand. "What would I do without you?"

"You couldn't get along," he said, "You know," he continued as if the idea were new, "maybe I should go along with you the first day. You haven't driven alone for awhile and these two," he nodded to Marty and True, "can be a handful—"

"Good idea," Chris Beth said, turning away. The real reason for his going along, she knew, was loneliness. She wondered anew what arrangements Wilson could make about the boy's education.

Probably, she thought as she flipped sourdough pancakes Young Wil had mixed, *it's all written down in Vangie's diary.* Had she given priority to the right items? Perhaps finding the key to the diary belonged under the heading of "urgent."

There was no further time for thinking. Morning chores finished outside, Joe and Wil came inside, bringing fresh milk to be strained, eggs to be stored, and appetites to be satisfied. True chose her favorite blue-plaid gingham dress for the first day then declared something was wrong with it...just as something was wrong with her bangs...Marty couldn't find his slate...and even Young Wil needed a button on the sleeve of his shirt.

Joe gathered up the breakfast dishes for her. "Can you manage?"

"I'll manage!" she said shortly. Regretting the tone, she turned to apologize but Young Wil beckoned Joe to help with hitching the horse to the buggy.

Wilson pushed his chair from the table. "Bring me the hairbrush," he said to True who was still fussing with her hair. "I'll help."

True handed the brush to Wilson obediently. Wiping crumbs from the table quickly, Chris Beth kept her eyes lowered. Hair needed a woman's touch and it hurt somehow to have Wilson offer to help. The gesture, like his closing the door to Vangie's bedroom, seemed so final.

"Ouch!" True's cry cut into Chris Beth's thoughts.

"Hold still or I'll use the brush where I think best!" Wilson's voice was teasing, but there was defeat in it—defeat and something else that was hard to define.

"Let me have it, Wilson," she said drying her hands as she crossed the room. "Your patients will be coming soon—"

"No patients."

Surprised, Chris Beth said, "But I thought you were opening the office again today—"

"No!" The single word cut across the silence with an emphasis that said more than additional talk. And yet she needed to hear more.

"Wilson—I—you—" Chris Beth fumbled for words that would say what she wanted them to.

"I'm tired of standing, Aunt Chrissy," True complained.

"I'm sorry, darling." Taking the brush from Wilson's hand, she fluffed True's bangs and curled the ends of the heavy braids. "Run and get the blue ribbons in the middle drawer of Mother's bureau."

When True hesitated, Chris Beth said, "It can be yours now."

"Mommy's and mine?"

"Mommy's and yours." Chris Beth managed to speak in spite of the enormous lump in her throat. Reassured, True skipped away like a small, golden butterfly.

"You see?" Wilson spread his hands out on the table, his right index finger tracing the intricate pattern of forget-me-knots Vangie had so daintily embroidered. "You see," he repeated softly, "why I must leave—"

"Leave!" The word was torn from Chris Beth's lips. "*Leave?*"

Wilson stopped tracing the embroidered design and clenched his fists. But he did not look up.

"There's no point in discussing it, Chrissy. I need away from the reminders—"

"We can put them away—I *promise*—"

Wilson's dark eyes raised to meet her own. There she read

pain, despair, and a certain consuming fire she was unable to identify.

"You can't put *these* away."

Chris Beth studied the hand that touched the bosom of his shirt. Strong. Sinewy. Filled with nervous energy. Gifted. Capable of tying tendons, but not hair ribbons. Able to mend bodies but not his own heart. Unwilling, even, to let others help. She had to try again.

"Time. It takes time, Wilson, and we all need each other—nobody can handle life alone—Oh, Wilson, *stay!*" Her voice broke then and without realizing that she was going to move, Chris Beth found herself kneeling beside him, her face against the rough worsted wool of his trouser leg. If only she could reach that secret part again—

"Don't, Chrissy—don't," he whispered, touching the top of her head gently. "Time can heal—some things—but this—" He pulled her head roughly against him. *"Oh, dear God, help us!"* And he pushed her away gently, rising from the table and helping her to her feet.

Then, Wilson, the doctor, was in control. Taking a white handerchief from his hip pocket, he shook it out and held it to her nose. "Blow!"

"I'm not a child!" she said, blowing furiously. Relieved to be back on familiar ground, even if it meant conflict, she smiled.

"That's better," Wilson said.

She turned away then, knowing that Wilson had left a lot unspoken. Maybe his decision was right for him. But what about the rest of the family? Wasn't it selfish of him to leave the rest of the decisions for them to resolve? Well, she had faced hardships before. She would face this one. And time, the gentle healer, would take care of everything somehow, no matter what Wilson said. . . .

11

Paradise Lost

True was right, Chris Beth reflected, as the wheels of the buggy rolled through the stretch of autumn woods within minutes of the school. It certainly was an extraordinary day—one which left no time for reassembling. Already the events of early dawn seemed unreal. Maybe they never happened. Looking back, she decided that her mind had been seeing mirages instead of reality throughout Vangie's illness. Fatigue would do that. Wilson wouldn't desert the children at a time when they needed him most. And what about his patients—the valley folks who depended on him to mend their bodies as they depended on Joe to heal their spirits? *No more thinking,* she admonished herself.

Not that there was an opportunity to think with both Marty and True chattering away like magpies. Did Marty see the orange pumpkins hiding behind the corn? Yes, and did True see how the stalks were bent like teepees? Maybe, the two agreed, Indians danced there at night.

Young Wil spoke above their excited voices. "Didn't Holmes refer to 'chill September'? How could anybody write that on such a day?"

"It was Holmes," Chris Beth smiled, her spirits lifting some. "And it was Lowell who claimed the rarity of June days. I guess neither of them saw Oregon in September!"

Surely, she thought looking around, *God is showing me something on this full-of-leaves day. Maybe it's new horizons of faith, greater hills of strength—or maybe He's testing the bedrock of my purpose—*

"Whoa, Dobbin!" At Young Wil's quiet signal, the aging horse stopped at the edge of the schoolyard and immediately the buggy was surrounded by children of all sizes.

Chris Beth inhaled deeply. The sky was clear and clean. The air was crisp without being chill, the wind free of dust. Young faces were filled with anticipation. And the nation's flag, bearing 33 stars, proudly striped the autumn sky above the newly-enlarged school building. Her sense of belonging, of reality, and of foreverness returned. Oh! It was good to be back.

Handing Marty and True over to the Malone children, Chris Beth turned to Wong Chu. "My goodness, Wong! You've grown another foot. So now you have three," she teased.

Wong's almond-shaped eyes crinkled with humor. "Which gives me a better *understanding*," he jested in return, his English precise and perfect. What a miracle! Five years ago the Chinese lad was little more than able to mouth a simple "Yes" or "No" other than in his native tongue.

"Come with me and I'll put the balls out—" she began.

A look of fear crossed the boy's face. "Wait! Miss Chrissy, there's a man inside, a stranger, who says, 'No admittance' each time I knock."

Chris Beth forced a tight smile. "The strange man is a new teacher, Wong. You can spread the word for me. And, Wong, will you explain to the other students that we must make him feel welcome?"

"I'll try," he promised. "And now the balls, please?"

"I'll get them," Chris said firmly. It might take some doing, but this man, schoolmaster, principal, whatever title he chose, had better brace himself for some compromises. She opened the door and went in.

"Good morning!" she called brightly, once the door closed behind her. Alexander Oberon stood at the front of what used to be the building's only room and would now serve as a gathering place when there were to be assemblies as well as housing the upper grades during the regular school day.

The new teacher turned quickly but took time to consult his vest pocket-watch before responding. "Good morning, Mrs. Craig," a frown in his voice matched the one on his face. "What time are you accustomed to arriving?"

"Earlier than this," she admitted, striving to keep irritation from her voice. "It was a trying morning," she added, hating herself for feeling that it was necessary to explain. Who did he think he was anyway?

"May I suggest that you arrive at least an hour before we begin classes?"

Well, things might as well be set straight. "You may suggest anything you wish, Mr. Oberon, but I shall come and go as my schedule dictates."

A look of shock crossed the man's face. "I—I—" he sputtered.

But, realizing she'd seized an advantage, Chris Beth said quickly, "I'll set the playground equipment out for the children, then we'll need to do some planning."

Shouts of glee rose from the children when Chris Beth opened the door and placed the box of assorted balls, gloves, and bats on the step. *Hooray!* the shouts said. *Our teacher won!* Oh dear! She hadn't meant to divide loyalties. *I'll have to be more careful,* she thought.

"It was nice of you to hoist the new flag," Chris Beth said once she had covered the distance between them. Determined to make an effort at cooperation, she went on, "And that's a nice bulletin board! Usually, I get over here several days in advance of opening day, but there's been a death in the family."

The tall frame beside her seemed to relax a bit. "I understand. And, of course, the first day's hardest. Now, shall we divide the two groups according to age or gender?"

"You mean," she said incredulously, "separate the boys and girls?"

"Precisely." Chris Beth saw then that Mr. Oberon wore a full, flowing tie, but at least he'd chosen ordinary trousers and a less formal coat.

"Does Mr. Goldsmith know about this division?" she asked.

"His idea, ma'am."

Well, there was no fighting the two of them. "Given a choice, then, I suppose it's best that I take the smaller children."

Something resembling a smile crossed the man's thin face. At least, she'd said *something* right. "Very wise." And the way he said the words, he might as well have rubbed his hands together in delight.

"By the way," Chris Beth said, as she helped him sort the books and put into separate stacks for the children to carry, "I plan to start my son and my late sister's daughter in a beginner's class. They'll be younger than the others, but—"

Mr. Oberon blew dust off his pile of books. "I foresee no problem" he said, fanning at the dust he'd blown into the air. "I plan to start an upper-grade class as well. There are at least six students registered now who are ready for a higher education."

Chris Beth straightened. "You mean—" Her heart beating so heavily against her ribs that it was hard to go on. *"Ninth grade?"*

"Ninth grade." Mr. Oberon's head bobbed up and down as he spoke, his Adam's apple bouncing like his head. "There's tentative approval from Salem, Mr. Goldsmith tells me—although I must say that change comes slowly here in the backwoods. Still," he granted, glancing at Chris Beth as if really seeing her for the first time, "they *did* hire a married woman, which is, to say the least, progressive. And generous."

Chris Beth opened her mouth then closed it. *Backwoods?* Mr. Goldsmith would straighten that one out before the year was finished. And, as to her employment—she shrugged. What did it matter what this newcomer thought? He'd learn. Beginning today! Anyway, there was little he could say or do that would destroy her elation over the addition of a ninth grade. What wonderful news for Young Wil!

She realized suddenly that Mr. Oberon was speaking and that she had missed the first part. "—so if you can sing in tune and will follow along?"

Dismissing the idea of telling this pompous man that she

was a soloist, Chris Beth said with false modesty, "I can sing in tune."

"Good! Then I shall lead while accompanying with my mandolin."

Well, that should be some feat, she thought, turning away with a smile. Her irritation was rapidly giving way to amusement. Why, she wondered suddenly, didn't his obvious disdain of women hurt her as she'd been hurt by Wilson's needling about her "Southern-belle helplessness" when she first came to the settlement?

Resolutely, she opened the turquiose- and rose-enameled case of her pendant watch then snapped it shut and secured it back into the ruffles of her blouse with the gold chatelaine. To compare Alexander Oberon with Wilson North was ridiculous—especially in terms of feelings. Wilson had aroused her ire because she *cared* what he thought. While Joe—well, Joe, gentle, loving Joe, was different from either of the other two men. *My husband,* she thought with a warm surge of affection, *does not search out my Achilles' heel. He loves me as I am.* . . .Chris Beth brought herself back to the classroom with a start.

"We should be calling the children. Should I ring the bell?"

"*I* will!" Mr. Oberon drew himself up full-height and marched to the door as if who rang the bell were a matter of great importance.

It took awhile to line the boys and girls up to his satisfaction. Filled with the very exuberance of living, they found much to talk about and giggle about. Obviously curious about the new teacher, they were even noisier than usual. It had taken Chris Beth five years to gain their full confidence and respect. Mr. Oberon expected to accomplish the same relationship immediately with rigid discipline. Well, she wished him lots of luck. He'd made it clear that her services were unwelcome so she would make no effort to intervene.

"Chins up, chests out, and straight forward! One word or one twitter will bring three raps of the ruler across the palm!" he said sharply.

Brown eyes, blue eyes, gray, green, and all the shades

between looked startled and then sought her face. Chris Beth tried hard to hide her distaste. Surely a smile would do no harm. She was wrong.

"And no smirking!" Mr. Oberon ordered when the children returned her smile.

Once inside and seated, the children were pin-drop quiet. "Atten*tion!* Class, rise—all together—and we will salute our nation's flag."

Young Wil's hand went up. "One of them leads," he suggested.

The way he said "one of them" told Chris Beth that Young Wil, as yet, did not know that he was among the group. Oh, she hoped that the new teacher did not alienate himself from this one. Like his uncle, Young Wil was a "still water" person.

Mr. Oberon eyed the boy. "*Used* to lead!" he corrected.

When Young Wil turned palms up in surrender, she breathed a sigh of relief. The others, watching the example, turned palms up beneath their scarred desktops then stood and, hands on their hearts, saluted in singsong.

"We read the Bible next," one of the boys up front whispered.

"No speaking without permission, young man! And *I* read a passage after group singing."

Taking a pitch pipe from his vest pocket, Mr. Oberon put the instrument to his lips and blew. The result was something akin to a nasal snort—a relationship not lost on the children. They burst into laughter. When the teacher responded with harsh words and threats of removing one recess, maybe all recesses of the day, Chris Beth realized that the matter was out of hand. Knowing that her actions would lead to displeasure, she rose from where she was seated at the back of the room and went quietly to stand beside Mr. Oberon. Immediately, the laughter stopped.

To her surprise, he handled the situation well. "Thank you for joining me, Mrs. Craig. We're ready for group singing."

Reaching behind him, he lifted a black, morocco leather case from the floor, unlatched it, and removed a beautiful mandolin from its flannel-lined resting place. There were "oh's" and "ah's" from all the children which Mr. Oberon chose to ignore, picking up a tortoiseshell pick instead, strumming a few bars and, to her dismay, sang out in a series of notes in the diatonic scale. "Do-do re-re fa so la!"

At the first sounds of laughter, Chris Beth put a warning finger to her lips. If Mr. Oberon saw, he gave no indication. "All of you will learn to sing like that!" he promised.

There was no enthusiasm. Neither did the children seem inclined to sing.

Chris Beth wished fervently that they could get on with classes, but there was more to come even after Mr. Oberon ignored the requests for the Twenty-third Psalm and read an obscure passage from Job.

"I sometimes read at the close of the day. Today, however, since we are assembled, I shall read from John Milton's *Paradise Lost.*"

The smaller children began to fidget. The older ones looked perplexed. Both signs were lost on the reader who seemed to enjoy the sound of his own voice.

When at last the reading was finished, Mr. Oberon raised his long-fingered hand for attention. "Chart class through fifth grade will follow Mrs. Craig through yonder door," he said. He paused significantly before adding, "Sixth through ninth remain."

"*Ninth!*" At least, Chris Beth saw no irritation when the whoop came from the several boys and girls who had come back nostalgically for one last look at the building and their friends before terminating their education. Mr. Oberon looked pleased at the enthusiasm.

She gave Young Wil's hand a squeeze in passing. He squeezed back appreciatively.

Once inside her own room, Chris Beth engaged the children in a game which allowed small legs to exercise. Then she told them in simple language the story behind *Paradise Lost.*"

"What's a paradise?" Jimmy John, youngest of the Malones, asked.

"The Garden of Eden, huh, Aunt Chrissy?" True spoke out as she was accustomed to doing at home.

"The Garden of Eden," Marty repeated.

"Then how could anybody lose it?" Jimmy John asked reasonably.

"Let's get to our ABCs now," Chris Beth said, closing the matter. They were too young to understand about losing *sight* of the Garden.

The rest of the day went well in both rooms. Chris Beth's little charges were eager to learn and Young Wil, once he heard the good news of the added grade, handled his new teacher with tact.

"He'll learn!" Young Wil laughed as Dobbin jogged lazily along at the close of the day. "And wait till I tell Uncle Wil about ninth grade! That should do away with his ideas of—of taking me with him—"

"You knew?" Chris Beth asked.

"I suspected, so I asked. I guess it's for the best—feeling the way he does." Young Wil urged the horse forward with a cluck then said slowly, "He hurts a lot and besides he wants to study some more about diseases—pathology?"

Chris Beth nodded and then asked, "Because of Vangie's illness?"

"Partly—then I think he just wants away—maybe from us all. Oh, Chrissy! You won't let him take True?"

The idea hadn't occurred to Chris Beth. Now fear clutched her heart. Oh, she mustn't let that happen! There had to be another way. Of course, if Wilson had his mind set . . . oh, not *another* conflict!

"I'll talk with him," she murmured.

There was no opportunity during the evening. No opportunity even for Young Wil to say much regarding the news. True and Marty monopolized the conversation. "And we heard about *Paradise Lost*!" True said as she kissed Wilson good night. "And Aunt Chrissy understands."

"*Paradise Lost*," he said slowly. "I wish I understood, too."

12

Promise of a Rainbow

Two weeks after school opened Wilson prepared to leave for Portland. They had been busy for weeks and Chris Beth was glad. Busy minds did not brood. Brooding would not bring Vangie back anymore than it would stop Wilson from leaving, she thought bitterly. Joe could be right. Maybe she did expect too much of a recently-bereaved man. But wasn't Wilson expecting too much, too, she asked herself between listening to the guttural noises of children trying to master phonetic sounds of *McGuffey's Readers* at school and holding mornings and evenings together at home. Wilson wasn't free. After all, he had a family to think about . . . and what about his practice? Then, resolutely, *I won't think about it.*

The late September rain moved out after clearing the summer haze from the sky and October came with a burst of glory. Bright leaves, bringing back memories of other autumns to Chris Beth, dropped one by one until the vine maples stood in deep pools of their own glory. Goldenrod flamed and milkweed offered bolts of silk to every teasing breeze. Chris Beth looked at the beautiful valley and felt that yesterday lay all around her. Gone was the growth of spring, the maturity of summer, and September's ripeness.

"It's evening of the year," she said sadly to Joe on one of their rare moments alone.

Joe took her hand. "But evening means stars, then dawn of another day."

Chris Beth tried to take comfort in his words, but a part of her reached out. Beyond the realm of too-busy days, the too-sad past, and the too-uncertain tomorrow. She needed something more reassuring—something perhaps she could find if there were a margin of time in her day to see October through the eyes of the forest . . . listen to the trees' soft whisperings . . . watch squirrels at their hoarding . . . letting her mind and muscles relax and just *be*.

"If I could escape and feel the world about me and see it, I could understand and become a part of its big rhythm instead of all the little humdrums of my day!" Over and over she said the words, knowing how futile they were. They would only bring her back full-circle to the realization that she belonged here, she *wanted* to be here . . . why, then, the sense of longing? Did other women feel this way? Probably not . . . but maybe they didn't listen to the wild geese calling at night . . . or try to convince a man like Wilson that he should stay here when, deep down, she might be wishing she were going away, too . . . .

Yes, it was good that she was busy! Nature's pace might slow in autumn. But for valley folk it was not yet time for leisure. There were fences to mend, fields to tidy, and gardens to bed down for the winter. And for Chris Beth there were inquisitive minds to satisfy at school and a family to hold together at home. *So*, she told herself firmly, *stop acting like a schoolgirl!*

And, blessedly, school was going well. Mr. Oberon, once he had "laid down the law," laid down the stick as well. Even Nate Goldsmith who was a firm believer in "lick 'em and larn 'em," ventured to say that the "Yankee gent was maybe goin' a piece too fur." But, "One o' these days you'll show 'im that he'll be catchin' a site more flies with sugar than vinegar!"

Well, it was stretching a point to say that she was responsible, Chris Beth knew. But, whatever accounted for the change, she was grateful. Now *home*—home, she thought a little hopelessly sometimes, was another matter . . . .

"Will Daddy be home for Thanksgiving?" True wondered. *Better ask Daddy. Aunt Chrissy doesn't know.*

"Who'll be taking over Uncle Wil's practice—till he comes

back? He *is* coming back, isn't he?" *Better ask Uncle Wil.* . . .

Chris Beth did know, however, that Joe had spent many long hours with Wilson and was sure that, as close as the two of them were, Wilson had told him a great deal more than she knew. Joe told her only that Wilson was arranging for a Dr. Mallory to see his patients.

"Here?" she had asked, hoping not. This house needed no more commotion than it had already.

"Oh, no," Joe reassured her. "He has an office in Centerville now. I'm not sure about house calls though."

And maybe even more important was the fact that settlers would have to drive for miles for a doctor's services, she'd said. But not forever, Joe had answered. *No, not forever. . .nothing was forever.* . . .

More storing, packing, rearranging. Another bedroom door closed. And another member of the family circle about to leave. Only "temporarily," of course. With all her heart, Chris Beth wished neither Joe nor Wilson would use that phrase gain. Life was too precious to spend doing *anything* temporarily. One must live every moment as if it were the last. Indeed! It might be. Time was no longer friendly.

"Well," Wilson said, rising from a squatting position where he had been sorting out enough emergency instruments to fill his doctor's kit, "that does it, I guess."

"Would you like a box lunch to take with you on the stage?" Chris Beth asked. "I've fried chicken—"

"Sounds wonderful, but you know our Miss Mollie. The stage leaves from there at twelve and she'll insist on feeding us a square meal before we board."

"You'll write?" Chris Beth asked.

"And send me a picture of the big hotel?" True broke in.

"Yes, Chrissy. And, yes, True."

Joe and Young Wil finished loading in Wilson's box of books and his one trunk. Coming inside, they joined Wilson, Chris Beth, and the two younger children. There was so much to say. Yet, there was nothing at all. The six of them stood awkwardly in the front room which had grown suddenly dark.

"It's going to rain," Joe said in surprise when there was a sudden clap of thunder. "I saw the little clouds earlier—"

Then without additional overture, there was a sprinkle of rain. Not much. Just enough to give the world a good-earth smell. And, then, astonishingly, there was sunlight.

"What do you know?" Wilson exclaimed. "Our Oregon storm is over!"

"There ought to be a rainbow!" True ran to the window with Marty at her heels. "Look, Daddy! It sucked up the colors from Mommy's zinnia bed."

Wilson turned toward Vangie's daughter but not before Chris Beth saw him wince in pain. But his voice, when he spoke, was steady.

"Look at that," he said in wonder. "They say rainbows have one foot planted in the garden and the other planted in heaven."

What a lovely thought! Chris Beth had never heard it before. The words were unlike Wilson, but he was filled with surprises.

"Is there really 'n truly a pot of gold at the end, Uncle Wil?" Marty wanted to know.

Wilson smiled. "O'Higgin says there is. Where's my spade?"

True giggled. "He's teasing, Marty. But, Daddy, isn't the rainbow God's promise?"

"It is," he said gently. "He promises never to destroy the world with a flood again."

"I like it when you talk like that," the little girl said, then tugging at his hand, "can't we go out and stand in it? Maybe God will promise *us* something special."

"We'll try it," Wilson said, picking up his kit. "Another thing O'Higgin says is that it's the 'luck o' th' Irish' to stand at the rainbow's end."

Wilson lead True and Marty to the flower bed in the front yard. Chris Beth felt such a lump in her throat that she didn't want to risk crying. She stayed behind the others, watching through the thin, white curtains. A tear spilled down her cheek and then, unexpectedly, she felt the warmth of Joe's arms from behind her. Depend on Joe to be at her side. And, yet, as she watched the others through a maze of color, Chris Beth had a strange feeling that she and Joe should have joined them. It was a wonderful way to say good-bye—beneath the promise of a rainbow. . . .

13

The Diary

Wilson left two messages. Not notes. Just reminders. But Chris Beth saw neither of them until several days later. She was too busy watching for signs of heartbreak that True might show. Losing her mother and then her father surely were too much for the young mind.

"Something has to give," she said worriedly to Joe.

"Not necessarily," he said. "Did she tell you about the rainbow?"

When Chris Beth said no, Joe went on, "She's convinced that the Lord made them a promise out there in the yard—a promise that Wilson will be back. Oh, for the faith of a little child!"

Chris Beth bit her lip in concentration. "I'm not so sure," she said uncertainly. "She could be very hurt by this. At this formative stage of her faith—"

Chris Beth paused, uncertain as to where one drew the line. "Just pray for his safe return," Joe said gently.

And Joe was right. Praying did help. It seemed like a sign her prayers were heard when Chris Beth saw Wilson's first message that he would be coming back to resume practice. At least, she took it as such.

Sweeping off the front porch on Saturday morning, Chris Beth raised the broom over her head and brushed it across the front door in search of cobwebs. It was then that she noticed Wilson's plaque still mounted to the left of the door. WILSON K. NORTH, M.D., the chiseled inscription read, as if his office were open for business.

"Joe, look!" she called excitedly to her husband who was sorting apples beneath the gnarled old tree where the children were picking the fruit for cider.

Joe selected two tree-ripened apples from the basket, polished them on his overall bib, and came to where she stood. Handing her one, he bit into his before answering. " 'Delicious' is the right name for these!" Then, smiling, he added, "I knew about the plaque."

Chris Beth bit into her apple. "Um-m-m," she said with appreciation. "This means that he really *is* planning to come back to stay—Oh, Joe, I hope he didn't just forget to take it down."

"He didn't forget, Chrissy," Joe said reassuringly. Then, when she did not reply, he added half-teasingly, "Come on now, 'oh, ye of little faith'!"

"It's not that exactly—Oh, I don't know how to explain."

How *could* she explain this feeling she had that the four of them who had become two now were only three after Vangie's untimely death? That the remnant of the family would never be reunited? Trying to shake off the sense of strange foreboding, she said, "How about some apple dumplings for supper?"

"Like I said, 'Delicious,' " Joe said, squeezing her arm.

"Not the Delicious apples," she said absently. "We'll need some Pound apples from the cellar."

Then, when Joe would have moved away, she detained him with a question. "Did Wilson discuss the children? I never did ask exactly how they came to stay—or what we should do in case—well, anything happened."

"Nothing's going to happen, Chrissy. But, to answer your questions, yes, we talked. He loves that nephew and step-daughter as if they were his own—which they are!"

Chris Beth nodded and he went on, "He would have taken them, however, if he'd had any permanent plans."

"I couldn't have stood that!"

"All the more reason to pray." Joe smiled and went for the apples.

That evening Chris Beth found Wilson's second message.

Vangie's diary! The thick, velveteen-covered book lay beside her best set of hairbrushes on top of the high chiffonier. And on top of her silver-scrolled hand mirror lay the small gold key that would open the book and reveal the messages meant for herself alone. Longing to open the diary and skim through the pages, and yet fearing to at the same time, Chris Beth tucked it beneath the linen sheets in the bottom drawer. She would open it tomorrow. No, tonight. No—*right now!*

Turning back the counterpane, Chris Beth sat down on the edge of the bed and fitted the small key into the lock of the diary. Almost reverently, she opened the first page and read the name, *Mary Evangeline Stein.* Vangie's maiden name! Then her sister had started putting down her thoughts long before her illness. Carefully, she turned the page to read the date in Vangie's delicate, spidery handwriting. The first entry was dated five years ago—almost to the day! Why, that would have been just before Vangie left their Southern home and came to the Pacific Northwest. With a shaking hand, she turned to the next page—at first tempted to skim the page, Chris Beth forced herself to read the words, so deeply-emotional for both of them, one by one. And one by one, the words tore at her heart.

> Dear Diary:
> It is with a pained but loving heart that I write these words. Actually, the words are not for you—or me—as much as for Others, two others. God, because the words confess my sins. And my beloved sister, whom I have wronged....

Gently, Chris Beth laid the diary on the bed beside her, facedown, to stare dry-eyed out the window at the last glow in the western horizon where the autumn sun had gone down. Evening meant stars, Joe had said, and after that the dawn. She wasn't sure. She wasn't sure about anything these days—even life itself, considering how Vangie's fragile breath, like a tiny candle, had fluttered and failed.

"I don't think I should read this," she said softly in the gathering dusk. "The words aren't meant for me."

Only, she knew better, of course. Vangie's last words had

been a request that she read the diary—abide by it . . . .

With an aching heart, Chris Beth picked up the book and tried to read it again, each word squeezing her heart a little drier.

> Word has reached me of Jonathan's accident and his death. I do not know what I shall do without Chris Beth and she is so far away—by miles and because of my folly. How can I ask her forgiveness? How can I tell her that the child I carry is Jonathan's, knowing that she and Jonathan were to have been married? And how—Oh, Dear Diary, how—can I make my mother and father understand? They will never believe that I loved Jonathan—my sister—them—or God. Maybe it would be better if I simply ended my life . . . .

With a cry of pain, Chris Beth laid the diary aside and gave way to a flood of tears. For the first time she realized what might have happened if she had followed her human inclinations and refused to accept her younger sister when their mother and her stepfather disowned Vangie and drove her from the family home. Some day she would read the rest of the heartbreaking diary. Some day. But not now. Now, she must say a long prayer of thanksgiving to the Lord who had arranged circumstances so that His will ruled over the human inclinations which would have ended in tragedy . . . and seek strength to go on.

14

Rebellion

Chris Beth had hoped that the hands of the clock would slow down once she had completed the tasks listed under "urgent." Instead, they seemed to pick up momentum as the October days sped past. Corn was in the cribs; stalks cut for fodder; apples were in the bins; all the canned fruit labeled and lined up neatly for winter. The hills filled up with wood smoke and other people seemed to find a bit of leisure. The slowing of their own time clocks pushed Chris Beth's ahead.

Added to the already overcrowded schedule was a growing sense of insecurity among the settlers. Folks needed a doctor closer 'n better'n them new ones in town. Old Doc Mallory had come to Centerville to retire, so they heard. Easy to tell he was a-mind to...had no memory a-tall and couldn't see his shadow without them spectacles he pinched on his nose. Shucks, he couldn't be up on the new way of doctoring. 'Course the other extreme was the likes of the "feisty feller" calling himself Dr. Spreckles. Too young to be a real doctor, he was. Too cocky, too. Mr. Oberon had never heard tell of such a school as he made claims of attending...probably one of them mail-order credentials. Nate Goldsmith granted that there just might be a few pint-size things even Alexander Oberon didn't know. He paused to look significantly at Chris Beth following a Sunday service and then continued, "But I wager he made a *D* when it comes to fixin' up liver ailments!"

Listening, Chris Beth supposed that she would have laughed behind her fan at such talk when she, Mama, and Vangie attended church back home. Or, more recently, perhaps she and Vangie would have looked at each other in amused tolerance under lowered lashes. But now—well, now their murmurings were disturbing.

Chris Beth expressed her concerns to Joe. He listened and then said, "Yes, I see it too. And besides—" he hesistated, lowering his voice, "I don't want the children to know, but there's a lot of friction between the Basque people and those living below."

"What kind of trouble, Joe?" Chris Beth was immediately alert. There had been an undeclared war between the sheep raisers and the cattlemen for years.

"Just unrest. One of these days things will explode. I'm going to have to spend more time calling on people—seeing if I can help mediate."

"Oh, Joe, we spend far too little time together as it is! I keep hoping things will slow down—"

"They will, Chrissy. You're doing a fine job and I often feel I neglect you in order to take care of the people's needs—"

"You are taking care of *God's* needs, Joe," she said loyally.

Joe had taken her hand that evening and pressed the palm to his lips. "It will all go better when Wilson finishes his courses in pathology and comes home."

If he ever came, she thought bitterly. She found herself half-wishing the courses Wilson planned to take would not be available or that something else would intervene so that he would return to help carry on here. So many people depended on him and Joe was so overworked.

"Joe," Chris Beth asked, suddenly remembering, "are you going to operate the mill alone?"

"Not alone. I'll have Young Wil."

Then came Wilson's telegram! The telegraph office was new in Centerville and whenever a "wireless" came through, the two "runners" continued to bring the exciting yellow envelopes to the recipients.

Back home, telegrams had meant bad news to Mama.

Shivering, Chris Beth watched Joe open the envelope, her memory going back to little-girl days when she stood wide-eyed watching her mother read the words and, more often than not, burst into tears without sharing the contents with Chris Beth. But, of course, one of those telegrams did bring the shattering news of her own father's death. . . .

Breathlessly, she waited for Joe to read the telegram and then share its message. Instead, he read aloud: CLASSES ARRANGED—STOP—WILL STAY AWHILE—STOP—MAY SEND FOR WIL—STOP—RAINBOWS TO TRUE—STOP—LOVE—WILSON.

"That's good news," Joe said in a sincere voice. "Isn't it?"

Chris Beth could not bring herself to answer. "We'd better call the children," she said instead.

The two smaller children jumped up and down. "The *rainbows* means our promise!" True said over and over, dancing around the living room. Marty danced with her, probably not caring why.

But Young Wil stood aside, making no comment. "Of course, we'd better not plan on your going right away," Joe said to the boy. "Your uncle and I talked about this— the possibility of your joining him there. You'll be ready for tenth grade next year and—"

"I've *been* in school there before. Remember?" he said and stalked out.

"Well!" Joe looked at Chris Beth in surprise. "That's news."

"Not to me. Young Wil has unpleasant memories of Portland—his mother's leaving his father for another man."

"It's a subject Wilson seldom mentions to me. He's still hurt by it, too. He told you that she sent for Young Wil after Wilson took care of him but he was unhappy and came back?"

Yes, he'd told her. Chris Beth remembered with a smile her confusing the names and, sure that they were father and son, summoning Wilson to school. That the boy was Wilson's nephew, his sister's son, surprised her. But remembering the rest of Young Wil's history erased the smile from Chris Beth's face. . . his dislike of the big city school. . . his striving for recognition and acceptance in the little one-room school where she'd struggled that first year as his teacher

...and the final breakthrough when she'd won him over....

"You and Wilson are the only ones who can really get to him—I mean, the part he holds back like Wilson," Joe said.

And Wilson was not here. So it was her job. Fine, but how? *How* was she to smooth out his security blanket with Wilson tugging at its corners? Well, she would do the best she could. But she was unable to resist saying, "It's Wilson's responsibility."

Maybe nothing would come of it. Maybe Young Wil would adjust to the idea...no, Chris Beth admitted to herself, she didn't want that! He was too dear to her. Maybe Wilson would come home and no decision would have to be made. *Time would heal.* Her own words.

But time ran out. The day following arrival of Wilson's telegram Mr. Oberon asked if he might see her after school.

Chris Beth smiled at his formality. "You need not make an appointment," she teased.

"I would not wish to infringe upon your privacy," he said stiffly, "except in matters of extreme importance."

Alas! Alexander Oberon had taken her declaration of rights too seriously. Well, at least, they had achieved a workable relationship if not a total understanding.

What time did he wish to see her? *Immediately after school.* If it concerned one of the students, should she bring records? *No.* The man's reluctance to give an inkling of what the "matter of extreme importance" was about puzzled her.

Once the students had cleared the building, Chris Beth invented a task for Young Wil and asked him to keep an eye on True and Marty, promising not to be long.

Mr. Oberon came right to the point. "Something happened to Wil Ames today which greatly disturbs me. You're his guardian, I understand."

"That's close enough," Chris Beth answered, then asked anxiously, "what happened?"

"This," the teacher said. He spread a paper on his desk and smoothed it with quick, nervous fingers. The handwriting was unmistakably Young Wil's.

"The lad seems in possession of a fine mind, has asked provocative questions, and, *ahem!*, until today conducted himself like a gentleman."

Chris Beth picked up the paper with trembling fingers. "Will you explain this to me? I'm not sure I understand."

"An examination over what I thought he had mastered. And look at this!" Mr. Oberon's voice rose as it was prone to do when he was agitated. " 'Parse a noun,' the assignment was."

Chris Beth looked at the writing and was torn between amusement and concern. "*Dog* is a noun with his tail sticking up and his feet hanging down."

While the answer might be funny, the problem behind it was not. Chris Beth had been through this before. There was the "*naked* old Nakomis" phrase the boy had misquoted purposely from *Hiawatha*. She'd know then, as she knew now, that Young Wil was clowning because he was troubled. But he must learn not to be impertinent.

Quickly, she skimmed the remainder of the tedious examination. The idea that any student would miss every problem in any subject, even geometry which she struggled with herself, seemed pretty unlikely. But it was downright preposterous to think that *this* one would write "Don't know" beneath the science questions when he knew the genus and specie of every living thing, as far as she could determine. And grammar!

Chris Beth laid down the paper in despair. "He knows the parts of speech backward and forward," she said. "This is—"

"Most distressing, most distressing!" Mr. Oberon broke in.

"This is," Chris Beth began again, "a sure sign that the boy's troubled about his uncle's leaving. I'll speak with him."

How many times—how MANY times—I've said that lately, she whispered to herself as she hurried to where the children waited in the buggy. The problem came under "urgent" all right, but then there would need to be a right time.

The right time came as the buggy rolled almost silently over the needled trail that led through the strip of woods near the North house. Marty was chattering away like a nut-gathering squirrel when True interrupted with a silencing finger to her lips.

"Quiet," she whispered. "We're close to Starvation Rock."

Marty's eyes widened, obviously pleasing True who loved to grab his attention with her sometimes hair-raising tales. "Did the Indians *really* jump down—" Marty began.

"Down, down, down! Into the canyon. Because they were starving to death, huh, Wil?"

Young Wil smiled. "Yep, I guess they did. So say those more resourceful than we."

"Than *us*," Chris Beth corrected automatically. "Object of the preposition."

"Beg pardon, Teacher," the boy said teasingly. "*Than's* not a preposition the way I used it. It's a connective of the understood subject—*So say those more resourceful than we are resourceful!*"

Chris Beth looked at him in amazement. "So it is. Then how on this earth did you come to miss every single answer on today's test?"

Young Wil dropped his head. At that precise moment the buggy rolled into the clearing. A shaft of late-afternoon sun touched the pale, straw-colored head, but it brought no light to his eyes. There was a momentary sadness which turned to defiance as his chin went up determinedly. "I've lost interest in school. I want to be a monk!"

Chris Beth burst out laughing in spite of herself. "And you think *they* don't study?"

Marty joined the laughter. "I wanna be a monkey, too!"

Little True sat upright. "It's not monkey, silly! It's *monk*. Monks live—oh, never mind." Dismissing the matter, she turned to Chris Beth. "Wil's mad because Daddy wants him to come to Portland. And I'm mad, too. If he wanted anybody, it oughta be me—he's *my* daddy—" An unexpected sob interrupted her words.

And before the buggy came to a safe halt, True jumped over the wheel and ran inside the front door. Marty followed, wailing in sympathy.

"Oh, Chrissy! I'm sorry," Young Wil murmured in remorse.

"I'm sorry, too, darling," Chris Beth answered through tight lips, "about *everything*."

15

"He Loves Me—
He Loves Me Not!"

There was no mention of the incident during the evening meal. When Joe drew Chris Beth close in bed that night he said, "Want to tell me about it?"

Needing the warmth of his nearness, she snuggled close—grateful as always for his strength.

Joe's arms tightened around her. "Something *is* troubling you."

"Just one of the students," she murmured against his chest. "Nothing to worry about in a wonderful moment like this."

Things went normally at breakfast, too. Maybe the children were a little less talkative—or maybe Chris Beth only imagined they were. There was no further word from Wilson, but the telegram served to answer questions neighbors asked at church. Debating whether to open the matter again with Young Wil, Chris Beth decided against it. That's how relationships fold, she knew—a wrong word or a right word but at the wrong time. It would be best to stay in close contact with Mr. Oberon. It would be best, too, to see this thing through alone—not push her suffering off onto others...Joe...the smaller children...or her friends.

"How is Wil responding these days?" Chris Beth asked

Mr. Oberon when she felt sufficient time had elapsed.

Mr. Oberon fingered the stickpin in his necktie. "Satisfac-torily, but," he paused to motion ups-and-downs with both hands, "the lad's seesawing. And he wears a 'You-figure-it-out' expression."

Yes, she knew the expression very well. For the first time, Chris Beth felt a sort of sympathy for the teacher. And, she admitted inwardly, a certain respect. Alexander Oberon was trying in his own way to understand a complex situa-tion she hardly understood herself.

Days ran into weeks and suddenly it was November. It was a cold fall. There was a misty rain that made everything sticky to handle. The sky was always dark, giving the look of perpetual late afternoon. Joe, who made frequent calls on congregation members, settlers in the Basque section, and the cattle ranchers who were non-church goers, stopped for mail at the general store at every opportunity. Marty, who could outdistance True only when his watchful eyes spotted Joe's horse, always rushed forward to give Joe a welcoming hug. True always waited her turn with ques-tioning eyes. *A letter from Daddy?*

"Not today, sweetheart." Each report made Chris Beth sadder.

On one such evening in mid-November, True asked, "Uncle Joe, my daddy'll be home for Thanksgiving, won't he—for sure?"

"We hope so. But," he said evasively, "Portland's a long way."

Sensing the child's sadness, Joe said, "If the weather per-mits, let's all burn leaves tomorrow. Would you like that?"

An autumn bonfire! It was a seasonal ritual the children loved. Raking. Burning. Watching the colored smoke and trying to guess which color leaves were making the crimson-orange blazes.

Chris Beth was as excited as Young Wil, Marty, and True when the first pile was heaped high. There was always a sense of adventure when Joe bent to light the pile from underneath—even a little quiver of danger. Everybody gathered close to watch as a blinding flare of heat and fragrance filled the chill air. "Victory!" they all sang out and went to gather more leaves.

Chris Beth left the group to prepare hot chocolate. Joe joined her soon, saying he'd best skip the chocolate and go to his study. "It seems that I get around to other things and not my priorities," he said.

"Amen, Brother Joseph," Chris Beth smiled. "Goes for me, too."

When the bonfire died down somewhat Young Wil came in for his hot chocolate. "Shall I pour?" he asked.

"Yes, do. I'll sit down with you as soon as I take these mugs to our fireflies out there."

Chris Beth started across the kitchen, carrying a mug in each hand. Then, hearing a noise that sounded more like a scream than a whoop, she hurried across the living room. There she stopped in astonishment.

Marty, holding a long stick, was poking the base of the leaves to send an explosion of sparks and rekindled flame into the air. And, as the blazes leaped high, True was attempting to leap over the burning bonfire—her long skirt billowing out as if to dare the tongues of flame.

Sloshing the hot chocolate over her hands and onto the cabbage-rose design of the carpet in her hurry to set the mugs down, Chris Beth rushed out the door to stop the dangerous game. But not before she heard True screaming wildly, "He loves me—He loves me not!"

"True, darling—no!" Chris Beth cried, running forward to grab the tiny figure. "That's dangerous!"

To her surprise, True collapsed into her arms, burying her soot-covered face against her breast. "I know," she sobbed. "I know and I don't care. He's not coming for Thanksgiving—my daddy's not coming—"

16

A Beautiful Hope

Chris Beth could not withhold True's unhappiness as she had Young Wil's. Joe overheard and helped soothe the child who obviously had been grieving more than they knew until today. Now that the children's feelings were out in the open, she hoped Joe would sit down and talk to her.

Still shaken, she said, "Join me for chocolate—"

But, before the sentence was finished, Joe answered. "I need to work on my sermon. And then," he said thoughtfully, "I guess I'd better make a trip to the general store—supplies for the mill—" His voice trailed off as the door of his study closed behind him.

Disappointed and hurt, Chris Beth went back into the kitchen. Young Wil was gone. And the chocolate was cold. In a sudden need for release of pent-up emotions, she seized the mugs and hurled them into the dishpan of soapy water left from the breakfast dishes. With a heavy thud, the mugs struck their target, splashing water onto the window above, their flight leaving a trail of syrupy brown. There, that should make her feel better. But it didn't.

Joe had built a fire beneath the wash pot in the backyard. The first pot of laundry should be boiling. But there was the floor to scrub . . . pressing and mending to do . . . the ironing would have to go, much as she detested spending evenings at the ironing board . . . and what about baking, lesson plans . . . .

Tears of despair filled her eyes as she mopped up the chocolate trail from the kitchen floor. That was her own fault, but what about the remaining work? There always seemed to be something she could or should be doing to make the lives of her family happier and more content, something more important than her own needs. The routine things to keep them clothed and fed. And the not-so-routine ones, but nevertheless important, like burning leaves and being together. Didn't that "clothe and feed" them in another way?

"Then why, Lord," Chris whispered as she wrung out the mop, "do I feel guilty? Why do I feel as if I am cradling the people I love in my womb—trying to insulate them from hurt, pain, *reality?*"

She paused to look out the window, inhaling deeply the arid-sweetness of the smoke mingled with overripe apples which had clung to the trees too long. Swallowing hard, Chris Beth let her taste buds follow the bonfire's luminous haze down to the musky odor of foliage in the damp woodlands down along the creek banks. If only, if *only*, she could get away...have a moment to herself...but the thought made her feel guiltier yet.

"Forgive me, Lord, " she continued her almost inaudible prayer. "I need to get away. I need—oh, You know what my needs are—"

Chris Beth's lips stopped moving when there was the sound of quiet footsteps behind her. Before she could turn around, Joe spoke.

"I've been thinking, Chrissy—things have been very hard here—" He paused and in a strong voice asked suddenly, "Would you like to go to Portland?"

"Portland!" *Portland?*

She turned to all but crumple in Joe's arms. He laughed softly and held her close. "There's a great need for the children to see Wilson—for all of us to have a planning session. It's been long enough now since—since our loss. But, Chrissy," he paused to lift her face, push back the tendrils of hair from her forehead and plant a kiss at her hairline, "Most of all, I want the trip for *you.*"

"Oh, Joe, I know we can't afford it, but yes, *yes,* I want

to go—Oh, it's a wonderful idea—wonderful, *wonderful!*"

To ride on the stagecoach again...stay in a hotel...see a big city...after five years. Outside, the sky had turned leaden again. It would probably rain. The family wash might never dry. It did not matter. Let the gray clouds come. There was a cobalt sky beyond. A beautiful new hope filled her heart.

17

Anticipation

Chris Beth watched her golden niece standing at the mirror, her back arched as she tiptoed to see her reflection. As True swept her pale hair up off her slender neck, Chris Beth fastened it with a silver barette, and then let it fall loose in a cascade below her shoulders. Her big, violet eyes with heavy blonde lashes—so like Vangie's—like her little-girl body, were never still. Her life would be filled with romance, if only it were not cut short like her mother's.

Watching her, Chris Beth felt a deep-down ache of sadness. But the sadness was overlaid now with the newfound happiness the family had found. Anticipation was mounting. The air was charged. "We're goin' to Portland. We're goin' to Portland!" Marty sang over and over as he hopped from one foot to the other. But True was too busy at the mirror to join his "silliness." She was suddenly a young lady, making elaborate plans for winning the heart of her father who was already head over heels in love with her, Chris Beth knew—even before his letters came.

When Joe made the planned trip to the general store, he found Wilson's letters which somehow had bunched up in the mail. Thoughtfully, he had written a letter to Young Wil, True, and Marty and, of course, a separate one to Chris Beth and Joe.

Young Wil, white-faced, opened the envelope and then fumbled with the single sheet of writing it contained. It was easy to see that he dreaded to read the lines. He now talked openly about not wanting to go to the city again. But if the letter said come—

True, who was learning to read at an uncanny pace, ripped her letter open and read the words aloud stumbling very little. Daddy loved her. Daddy had found just the right gift...Daddy had seen another rainbow...it would bring him home...someday.

Marty, by far less mature than True, handed True the letter to read aloud to him. But he kept the envelope! Receiving a letter addressed especially to him was of much more importance than what the letter said.

Wilson wrote in much greater detail to Chris Beth and Joe, of course. The courses he was taking were difficult, his schedule heavy—which was good leaving "no time to think." There was no other reference to loneliness or grief.

"That's a good sign," Joe said when he finished reading the letter. "He's working his way through it." Then, picking up the letter again, "There's a postscript on the back," he said. "Did you see it?"

When Chris Beth shook her head, Joe read it aloud: "There's so little time. Had hoped for Thanksgiving with you but will have only the one day. And Christmas seems so far away."

"He won't have to wait!" True said happily and went back to experimenting with her hair.

Joe looked at Chris Beth in amusement and then lowered his voice. "Have you mentioned our plans to your principal?"

"Mr. Oberon loves that title," she smiled. "If I could use it somehow in making the request—and, to answer your question, no, I haven't. I guess I'm afraid to—like Young Wil was about opening the letter. By the way, what *did* it say?"

"I don't know, but nothing earthshaking, I guess. He seems fine."

Chris Beth hoped that she would feel fine—after tomorrow. Yes, tomorrow for sure she must approach her "principal."

When she approached Mr. Oberon the following day after

school, Chris Beth was surprised how willingly he listened to her request for a short leave and the reasons behind it. He kept nodding in encouragement and before she realized it, Chris Beth found herself confiding some of her misgivings—things she had kept carefully to herself.

"I understand completely," he said when she finished. "And I concur. Of course, as your principal, I may find it necessary to speak with the president of the board before reaching a decision. You understand?"

Chris Beth understood. But how did Mr. Oberon feel?

Mr. Oberon had taken charge of larger bodies of children than this before. Mr. Oberon could manage. As a matter of fact, Mr. Oberon said, with a squaring of his thin shoulders, that he had been thinking—just thinking, mind you—that it might be wise if one of them attended the Teacher's Institute held in Portland on Thanksgiving weekend. *Thanksgiving weekend!*

"Oh, Mr. Oberon, that would give us two whole days with our brother-in-law—put the family together—"

"It can be managed!" he said as if the matter were settled. "I am glad to help you out in time of trouble. Remember that, Mrs. Craig."

With a sudden rush of warmth, Chris Beth said, "Oh, please, when we are out of the presence of the children, can't you call me by my first name?"

Mr. Oberon's pale eyes met hers. They seemed to have lost the glint of cool arrogance that she felt was designed to provoke her.

"Thank you," he said as if acknowledging a first compliment.

Carried away on the wings of excitement, Chris Beth said daringly, "Then I think I shall call you Alexander—no, Alex. Has anyone called you that before?"

Alexander Oberon looked flustered. "No. *Alex*," he licked his upper lip as if sampling the word. "I like that. Yes, I like it very much!"

Chris Beth left him standing, still stunned, in the middle of the larger classroom and hurried out to tell the children the good news. Then the four of them urged Dobbin ahead so they could tell Joe.

"Well, it's all settled—except for the biggest part of all. Getting tickets on the stage and warning Wilson we're coming!" he smiled. "I'll ride over to Turn-Around Inn tomorrow, check schedules—"

"Oh, Joe!" Chris Beth interrupted, feeling reckless. "I have so much to do, but I haven't seen Mrs. Malone for ages and—"

When she looked questioningly at Joe, he said, "We'll get it all done. Come along that far."

But Mrs. Malone had other ideas. The air in her kitchen was heavy with peeled fruit and boiling vegetables in preparation for the evening meal. On top of the stove she was boiling a smoked ham. So dinner at the inn was under control, she said.

"Just gimme a minute t'leave a note for O'Higgin and I'll be comin' along."

The suggestion caught Chris Beth by surprise. "That would be nice," she murmured, "but I hadn't planned—"

" 'Course you hadn't," she said, wiping her hands on her apron, "but then you hadn't planned on goin'—and *that* calls for a brand spankin' new dress!"

"No—no, really—I mean, we can't afford more than the tickets."

"Amelia!" Mrs. Malone called up the stairs to one of her stepdaughters. "Bring down my winter felt." Mrs. Malone turned to look into the mirror above the hall tree as she smoothed back the strands of graying hair and tucked them into the practical bun at the nape of her neck. "You know, maybe you won't have t'scrounge around as much as you might think money-wise. Trustees pay *your* board 'n keep so that's one less ticket. We'll invest in some taffeta. You seen th' new dress shops?"

Chris Beth had not. Well, they sure beat the catalog-ordered one all to pieces. Custom-made? Oh! That would cost too much. Now, who was talkin' 'bout hirin' it done? Why, Mrs. Malone could take "one gander" at them shop windows and copy that French lady's work....

While Joe went to the ticket office to arrange transportation and send a wireless to Wilson, Chris Beth and

Mrs. Malone went into the general store to look for the right fabric for *The Dress*.

Mrs. Solomon, looking little changed from the raw-boned, somewhat domineering proprietress Chris Beth had met five years ago, stepped from behind the coffee grinder. "We grind for customers nowadays," she explained. "So what can I be doing for you ladies?"

While Mrs. Malone explained their mission, Chris Beth looked around, surprised at the changes. Fewer picks and shovels. More laces, buttons, and ribbons on the newly-oiled counters. The store, looking large since the three windows were added, still smelled of camphor; but it was less overwhelming since installation of the line of colognes marked: ESPECIALLY FOR MILADY'S TOILETTE!

"This calico would be practical for traveling," Mrs. Solomon said as she and Mrs. Malone joined Chris Beth.

"Not this time, Bertie," Mrs. Malone said. "Show us something in taffeta—less'n you'd rather we shopped around—"

"This way!" Bertie Solomon's words tumbled over each other as she swished through the bolts of dry goods.

Chris Beth's heart beat rapidly with excitement as she fingered the luxury of the waterfalls of taffeta in brilliant autumn colors. They were *all* so tempting—until she saw the indescribably beautiful color that seemed to come alive in her hands.

"Oh, this is it, Mrs. Malone! This is it!"

Mrs. Solomon cleared her throat. "The latest," she said with a quick eye for business. "Still and all, it's expensive—but worth every penny, wouldn't you say, to have the very newest? 'Ashes of Roses' it's called."

" 'Ashes of Roses' it's gonna be, Bertie. But put down them scissors till I've done a bit o' lookin' in Madam Francois's window. Then I'll not be needin' a pattern!"

Once Mrs. Malone was out the front door, Bertie Solomon turned to Chris Beth. "So you're going to see Wilson. Surprises folks around these parts he's not been home looking after his practice."

In spite of herself, Chris Beth felt a liquid trail of anger flood her chest. Bertie was Bertie, Mrs. Malone said—

"comin' through in time of trouble but prone to meddle."
How true!

"Wilson is in school, Mrs. Solomon—studying pathology."
Try as she would, the words were defensive.

Mrs. Solomon swung the scissors to and fro by the string
suspending them around and below her neck. "While people hereabouts could be dyin' off like flies," she clucked
her tongue. "Not proper he should be alone there in
Portland either—too eligible—and all the temptations of the
big city—"

"I'm sure Wilson can handle himself," Chris Beth said
stiffly.

"All the same it's good you'll be checking. Our Maggie
reports that he's well, but it's best you, well, look in on 'im."

The front door swung open to let Mrs. Malone enter, giving Chris Beth a chance to turn away before Bertie Solomon
could read the shock in her eyes. Maggie? Maggie was in
Portland? She had seen Wilson? Would Mrs. Solomon never
give up trying to match her daughter up with Wilson
North? How obvious could she get?

Surprise gave way to anger—as if the fire in her heart
had never died out where Maggie was concerned. Maggie,
the woman who had tried so hard to hurt Vangie with her
back-biting ways, would always fan a furious flame in Chris
Beth's heart. *Wilson was too busy to see his family. Wilson
was too involved in his studies to resume his practice.
Wilson's heart needed mending... but he was not too busy,
involved, or broken-hearted to see Maggie Solomon, this
"changed woman" who went back to her old ways....*

A little of the autumn glory went out of the day. A bit
of the anticipation went out of Chris Beth's heart. But she
determined not to let it show. They would go to Portland
as planned. And there she would have a very long, very
private talk with her brother-in-law.

18

A First Snowflake—
A Growing Fear

It was best, Chris Beth decided, to make no issue of the petty incident at the store. Why add a twist of lemon to Joe's plans? She and Mrs. Malone could discuss the ambitious mother and her 'When-I-would-do-good-evil-is-nigh' daughter (Mrs. Malone's apt description) when an opportunity presented itself. But when the older woman brought the partially-finished dress to the Big House for a fitting, Chris Beth felt that it would be a shame to spoil the moment with unpleasantries. Mrs. Malone was obviously excited. And when she lifted the "Ashes of Roses" dress from the faded newspaper wrapping, it was easy to see why!

"Oh, it's beautiful, *beautiful!*" Chris said again and again, holding the dress against her body.

Mrs. Malone's eyes glowed with pleasure; but there was a look of fatigue in their gray depths. Suddenly Chris Beth felt selfish. How could she have let this woman with a husband, six children, and keeper of an inn, always overflowing with guests in need of beds, baths, and meals, take on another project? As a matter of fact, she didn't have to have a new dress just because her own trip came as an unexpected stipend. The old guilt was back....

"Tell me now, how long you plannin' to sit there moon-eyed instead of modelin' my first "French creation'?" Mrs. Malone asked.

"I'm sorry," Chris Beth said quickly. "It's just that you have so much to do—"

"Th' good Lord gives me a hand. Now, get this dress on!"

Obediently, Chris Beth allowed Mrs. Malone's capable hands to slip the whispering folds of taffeta over her head, letting the soft luxuriousness caress her skin. Mrs. Malone had refused to reveal the secret of The Dress's style and Chris Beth found it difficult to stand still during the pinning session. What would it look like?

"Can't I look now—just a little peek?" Chris Beth begged.

"Y'er worse'n my Lola Ann, Amelia, 'n Harmony added up," Mrs. Malone complained, her words muffled by the mouthful of pins. "Lucky us folks today don't have t' keep others standin' while we stick a garment in place. Turn a bit to th' right."

Chris Beth turned. " 'Most finished," Mrs. Malone said. "Time was, y' know when we had no pins. Turn!" Waiting for Chris Beth to turn, Mrs. Malone talked on, "Had only one needle here in the settlement when Ma sewed my clothes. Used to share with folks around us. Us kids took the needle for patchin' from one homestead to th' other. Our Ma's threaded th' precious piece of steel with red yarn and stuck it in the eye of an Irish potato—once we lost it— like I lost my listenin' audience, it's plain t' see. All right, go ahead, child, and have yourself a look!"

Chris Beth ran to the full-length mirror above the lowboy in the adjoining room. There she stopped in absolute awe at the reflection she saw.

The demurely-high, lace-edged stock collar offset by daringly-short, three-quarter length sleeves...the bolero effect made by Valenciennes lace and insertion stitched onto the bodice...the high-style tucks nipping in the waistline...the exciting skirt made with front panel and wide, wide fullness at the sides. Chris Beth whirled around as if dancing to silent music, causing her cheeks to take on a rosy glow—the exact shade of the beautiful gown.

In a burst of excitement, Chris Beth cried out, "Oh, Mrs. Malone! I'm beautiful—"

Then, embarrassed, she stopped short. But Mrs. Malone picked up the conversation matter-of-factly. " 'Course you are, but th' dress didn't create it—just let it show."

Then, picking up a spool of thread and three fallen pins, Mrs. Malone put them into her pin cushion, tucked it in her paisley bag, and said, "Let me help y' out of the garment. O'Higgin's probably chompin' at the bits of loneliness—or scarin' the young'uns stiff with them Spook Hollow tales brought over from Ireland," she said affectionately.

At the door, Chris Beth paused before saying good-bye. "Mrs. Malone, you *do* think it's proper for me to be going to Portland?"

"To see Wilson? Well, of course!"

"No—I mean, on a pleasure trip—so soon after—"

Mrs. Malone sighed. "Chris Beth, it's been almost three months since our Vangie left us. Life goes on. Or could it be," Mrs. Malone asked suddenly, "that what you're really wonderin' is if you oughta be wearin' black?"

"Well," Chris Beth admitted, "I did wonder if the color was too bright."

"Humph! Think Wilson won't be needin' that? Me, I never was one for long faces and shrouds! I plumb refused a black shawl for my head when I lost my Mr. Malone, rest his soul. Wore me a green bonnet instead. And you know what? O'Higgin spotted it that very day—and in due time, well, you know the rest. We just never know what the Lord has in His pocket, but 'tis always better'n we expected."

Chris reached out and embraced Mrs. Malone, wondering what she would do without her. For a moment, they held each other in the kind of silence between women that says more than words. Then, Mrs. Malone opened the door to let in a gust of late-November air which had grown suddenly chill. And how had the sky darkened without their noticing?

Mrs. Malone climbed into the buggy then called, "Well, what do you know? A first snowflake—pretty early, I'd say. Best I hurry!"

Waving good-bye, Chris Beth closed the door quickly,

wincing as the cold air it fanned poured over her, seeming to seep to her bones.

Usually, she welcomed the snow along with the children. But not today. If it stuck . . . well, she mustn't think like that. All the same, she could not resist going to the window to peer through the drapes. Maybe the lonely little flake was all. But no! Big, soft flakes were melting against the glass. Any minute now, if the temperature dropped, they would stick.

Chris Beth turned from the window, her sense of elation gone. Somehow she knew that she would never wear *The Dress*—the beautiful "Ashes of Roses" dress.

19

Emergency!

With an enthusiasm she did not feel, Chris Beth called upstairs to where Young Wil was tutoring Marty and True in their vowel sounds, "Dismiss your class, and come see the snow!"

"We saw it a'ready," Marty called back morosely.

When the trio came down, there was no spring to their steps, no excitement in their voices. They loved snow, but it could close the roads.

Still trying to dispel the gloom, Chris Beth said to True, "My mother, your grandmother, used to say when it snowed that Mother Goose was picking her goslings for stuffing pillows."

True eyed her gloomily. "My mummy said the feathers came from angel wings. I like that better. *She's* an angel now—my mummy is—huh, Aunt Chrissy?"

Chris Beth hesitated. "I don't know a lot about angels, darling," she said slowly. "I believe they're especially created—"

The child shook her head slowly from side to side. "My mummy's an angel. She's my angel-mother. These feathers could be hers—"

An enormous lump formed in Chris Beth's throat. It was with great relief she heard the door of Joe's study open. But before she could welcome him into the group, there was a knock at the front door.

"Brother Joseph! Brother Joseph!" a man's frightened voice called without waiting for an answer to his knock.

Darkness had settled over the valley. But a different kind of darkness settled over Chris Beth's heart. A strange premonition—worse than any she had ever before experienced—gripped her entire being, paralyzing her so that she was unable to move. It was Joe who had to hurry across the big living room and open the door.

Ruben Beltran, one of the Basque sheep raisers, stood shivering in the darkness. His hair was disheveled. He wore no coat. And there was the unmistakable stain of blood oozing from his left shoulder. Blood!

Oh, dear Lord! Chris Beth's numbed mind could pray no further. As if in another world, she heard Mr. Beltran's incoherent words. Shooting . . . cattlemen first . . . then vigilantes taking "law and order" in their own hands had joined the masked men . . . crosses burned in yards . . . burned Ole Tobe's house . . . determined to get "black blood" out of the settlement . . . slaughtered his sheep . . . .

"Inside before you freeze, Mr. Beltran," Joe urged gently as he ushered the man in and closed the door. "Is Tobe all right?"

"Not killed, but left with a wandering mind after losing his Mandy short while back. Oh, Brother Joseph, come—come *now.* It's my Liza. She's shot!"

Little Liza! Chris Beth felt a wave of nausea sweep over her. Liza, the beautiful little 8-year-old cripple who was unable to travel the long distance to school daily but visited sometimes and was a member of Chris Beth's Sunday school class.

"They wanted a '*human* sacrifice,' they said," Mr. Beltran sobbed. "Called her my 'sacrifical lamb'—my Liza—"

Chris Beth forced her leaden feet to move, forced her limp hands to reach for the sheep raiser's work-calloused ones. "I'm so sorry—so sorry," she whispered through frozen lips.

Sympathy she would offer. Hot coffee . . . and she would bind up his wounds with the gauze and disinfectant Wilson had left for emergencies . . . then tomorrow she would visit . . . .

But even as the thoughts crowded through her mind with confusion, Chris Beth knew what would happen. She would turn around to see Joe donning his heavy coat, buckling his boots, picking up his Bible.

"No!" The word forced its way from her lips. "Joe!" She ran to her husband, clutching at his arms to keep them from pushing into the wool windbreaker. "Don't go—not tonight—don't get involved—"

When Joe pushed her hands from his arms gently, her panic turned to hysteria. "You *can't* go! Don't get mixed up in their quarrels. Let them settle it. You—you're a minister—not a doctor or sheriff—or a judge! *A minister!*"

"Which is why I have to go, my darling. I won't be long, I promise. Lock the doors and try not to worry. We'll be together soon, I promise." He kissed her tenderly and was gone.

As if in a trance, Chris Beth watched the two men mount horses and ride away in the gloom. The snow was beginning to stick, her dazed mind noted. Joe was gone—gone as he's never left before—gone to settle a shooting. Gone without a last word of love from her . . . and she hadn't even offered to bind Mr. Beltran's wound. What good were their years here anyway? The valley was more troubled than before she, Joe, Vangie, and Wilson had dedicated their lives to it.

Suddenly, she was on her knees. "O Lord," she cried out in the words of David. "How long wilt thou be angry against the prayer of my people . . ." Her prayer dissolved into dry sobs of despair.

20

A Distant Prayer

Chris Beth rose from her knees at length, but the peace she had hoped for had not come. Uneasily, she peered into the darkness again. It was still snowing and the flakes were smaller. That meant the snow would stick. As she replenished the wood in the fireplace, she wondered where Young Wil could have taken Marty and True. She remembered vaguely that Joe had cautioned the older boy to look after the family while he was gone. Wasn't that unusual—for such a short trip?

Forcing her mind another direction, Chris Beth prepared tomato soup and cornbread. At the sound of feet on the back porch, she opened the door to find Young Wil standing with milk pails in his hands. The two younger children, carefully muffled in their snow clothes, walked behind him—each swinging a lighted lantern.

Surprised, she stooped to kiss them both and give Young Wil a look of appreciation. "Come in," she said quickly. "Get your mittens off and we'll have supper in front of the fire."

They ate in near-silence, each buried in private thoughts. There was no need to force small talk none of them wanted, Chris Beth knew. Somehow she managed to hear their prayers, mostly pleas that the snow would stop, then she and Young Wil went downstairs to keep watch. Their concerns went deeper than disappointment. Joe's safety was at stake and they both knew it.

For a few minutes neither of them spoke. In the silence, Chris Beth heard the scrape of a branch against the west window. That meant the wind was rising. Snow would drift over the roads, hiding them...and somewhere out there her husband was fighting to save lives...maybe his own. The fire crackled again and she tried to concentrate on the comforting warmth of the flames. But something happened to her vision. Her eyes went out of focus. The flames blurred. And in their place she saw a field of snow, drifted in waves sculpted by angry wind, piled high against the trees—*melting in pools of blood!*

Raising a hand to her mouth, Chris was barely able to stifle the cry of horror that began in her throat. Then, mercifully, Young Wil spoke.

"I never did tell you what was in Uncle Wil's letter."

"No," she managed, her voice trembling, "you never did."

Reaching into the breast pocket of his plaid shirt, he drew out a crumpled sheet of paper. "It's a prayer. My Uncle Wil wrote it. He's a writer, you know."

Yes, she knew. And even with the terror she was feeling, Chris Beth was able to detect the pride in Young Wil's voice.

"I'll read it if you want me to—it's good."

She nodded mutely.

> Loving Father, open my eyes and my heart that I may see this fair earth which You have created. Open my heart that I may feel this beauty pulsate through my soul. Let me see, let me feel, the warm joy in Your sunshine, the quietness of Your forests, the strength of Your everlasting hills. Through these, let me know that I am safely held in Your strong hands and be sustained by Your love. And, in time of storms, Lord, remind me that I am near nature's heart. Still my restless spirit. Remind me that the frozen brook, though silent, is running underneath and that the sleeping bulbs will awaken one day to become lilies of the field. And, for these storms, make my life better, stronger, more worthy—more aware that the Eye watching over the sparrow is watching over me.

Young Wil read the words clearly and beautifully. When he finished, Chris Beth was too overcome to speak.

"Did you like it?" he asked folding it carefully, and returning it to his pocket.

"I think it's one of the most beautiful prayers I ever heard," she said truthfully.

"Did it help? I mean—it always makes me feel better."

Yes, it made her feel better, Chris Beth told him. But she did not say how. It brought no peace—not the kind she needed. But the prayer Wilson had written added a new dimension to him. *Surely,* she thought, *a man who writes like that to a boy must have more understanding than I've allowed. Still, why isn't he here where he belongs? Why does he pray at a distance?*

"The man who brings peace to th' settlement can't be no outsider," Mrs. Malone had said when Joe was weighing his ability to minister here. "He has to be one of us who understands folks' ways and sets a good example even when Sunday's finished!"

That was well and good. But wasn't Wilson one of them, too?

21

All-Night Vigil

The fire was nearly out. The logs hissed in the grate and a pencil line of smoke trailed up the chimney. The room felt suddenly colder and Chris Beth wrapped her arms around her chest and held onto her elbows. "You'd better try and get some sleep," she said to Young Wil. "I—I think I'll read awhile."

When the boys long legs disappeared around the bend of the stairway, Chris Beth put another log in the fireplace and paced the floor restlessly. Outside the wind shrieked. It was easy to imagine such force blowing snow in horizontal sheets past the windows. She must do something—*anything*—to get herself under control. It was then that she remembered Vangie's diary. She would read through it until Joe came home.

Skimming what she had read before, Chris began anew:

> Today I told Mama about the child I am carrying. She will tell Father Stein and I am terrified of his wrath. Oh, if only I had Chrissy with me...my sister would forgive my every transgression...together we would talk to the Lord and I would be forgiven by them both....

Misty eyed, Chris Beth read on, stopping at points to stare into the corners of the big room where shadows tangled against the massive furniture as the logs in the fireplace shifted restlessly. Each time it was harder to return to Vangie's spiraled handwriting and read the broken-hearted messages which clutched at her own heart and squeezed it dry. But she forced herself to read on.

Vangie's father knew . . . pushed her from the house, calling her a "woman of the night" and saying that God would punish the baby . . . her lonely trip west after Jonathan's accidental death . . . and being reunited with "my beloved sister to whom I dedicate this book."

> But how can Chris Beth love me? I deliberately came between her and Jonathan—only then I did fall in love with him, deceiver though he was. . . I always envied my older sister, but I never meant to hurt her. How could I have been so fickle, so vain? But I have paid— oh, how I have paid! There are times, even now, when I take a good look at myself in the mirror and ask what would have happened had I not come here? Would love have bloomed between Wilson and Chris Beth . . . did I make the same mistake all over again? But enough rambling, I must set new day-to-day goals and look forward to the wonderful, long, *long* life which lies ahead for the four of us. . . .

Softly at first then in a swelling of volume the grandfather clock chimed the mellow notes of *"Tempus Fugit,"* a plaintive reminder that life for the four of them did *not* go on for a long, long time. Vangie, dear little Vangie, lay beneath the first blanket of snow. Startled by a new thought, Chris Beth sat erect to count the strokes of the clock's gong. *Maybe Joe was buried in this snowstorm, too. . .and Wilson was far away. . . .*

Three o'clock! Reason told Chris Beth that she should be in bed, but she was unable to leave the spot where Joe had left her. Reason told her that he would be all right. It would be foolish to ride back in the storm. He would stay with the Beltrans. . .but a force stronger than reason told her this wasn't so. Joe would be home as soon as possible. He had promised. Nothing would hold him back . . . unless . . . yes, something had happened . . . *something*.

To curb her wild imaginings, Chris Beth picked up Vangie's diary again. Once past the emotional prologue,

Vangie wrote on a day-to-day basis concerning her arrival... her enchantment with the beautiful Oregon Country and her love for its warm, gentle people.

After awhile, Chris Beth forgot that she was reading from the pen of her departed sister and it became a sad-sweet pleasure to taste again with her the excitement of their early days here. The pages filled up with their move into Joe's cabin—a doll's house, Vangie called it—the evenings around the fireplace where she sat now... only it was the four of them then, planning their weddings, spinning dreams like dew-pearled cobwebs that lasted but a single night... Wilson's acceptance of the baby... his claiming it for his own.

Some of the writing was too personal. It belonged to Wilson. Chris Beth wondered anew why her sister had insisted that it was she who should read it and follow whatever instructions lay somewhere within the pages. It was important that she read on, but she was so tired.

She leaned back wearily and dropped into a strange, restless world of sleep. In her dreams, Chris Beth was in a cramped room—airless, with sooty curtains hanging motionless over crooked window frames. Out! She wanted out! Wildly, she fumbled for a door which seemed nonexistent. Until suddenly it appeared right in the center of the dream and opened for her by an unseen hand. And there before her lay a beautiful garden, sun-splashed and green-carpeted, with purple waterfalls of wisteria cascading over the high stone walls. There were no faces, but she knew the voices! Joe, Vangie, Wilson calling for her to join them. The door was open. Why then was she unable to pass? Instead, she crashed into an invisible wall.

Damp with perspiration, Chris Beth came slowly out of the dream. Burnt orange flames were crackling around three newly-stacked logs before her. A long arm reached out with poker in hand to adjust them.

"Joe!"

"He's not here yet, Chrissy," Young Wil said softly. She tried to sit up. "What time is it?"

"Six thirty. The milking's finished and I have coffee for us."

"Oh, darling, you're wonderful," Chris Beth said, licking her dry lips and trying to remember clearly events of the preceding night.

Stiffly, she drew herself up, sensing immediately that something in the room was different. There was a peculiar, glaring quality to the faint rays of dawn—a certain brightness that she knew could not be artificial. And yet it couldn't be the beginning of sunrise either.

Pulling her woolen robe around her, she went back to the east window. And, with sinking heart, she saw a world gagged by snow.

Young Wil joined her at the window. "I'll saddle Dobbin right after breakfast. Don't you think I should ride over to the inn?"

"I don't know—I just don't know. I'm so worried," she confessed, "but I don't want you taking chances. Look!"

She pointed a shaking finger at three figures, apparently wearing snowshoes, moving slowly toward them in the dim light. It was strange, she was to think long, long afterward, how neither she nor Young Wil rushed to meet the men. Somehow, they knew something was wrong.

22

"We Be Comin' To Tell You . . ."

Three men with grim faces. O'Higgin, Nate Goldsmith, and Alexander Oberon stood hesitantly at the front door.

O'Higgin, his usually ruddy face pale even against the whiteness of the snow, was first to speak. "We be comin' to tell you—"

The booming voice broke. He was unable to go on. The other two men stood statue-still, silent in sorrow.

"It's Joe, isn't it?" Chris Beth was unable to recognize the voice that must be hers.

O'Higgin nodded and shook his head to indicate that he was unable to speak more than the single word, "Accident."

He didn't need to. Chris Beth knew. She had known all along.

"*Accident?*" The voice of Young Wil, who had come to stand behind her, was no more than a horrified whisper. "What kind of accident?"

None of the men answered. They simply stood like actors in a pointless play who had forgotten their lines. And she, the main character in this tragedy, would have to prompt them.

"Joe's dead," she said woodenly.

They spoke then, the three of them at once. It was a mistake . . . a terrible mistake. It was easy to make mistakes in horrible mixups like there had been . . . they—nobody would even know whether it was a drunken cattleman, sheep rancher, or vigilante—fired wildy. But Joe wasn't hit, ma'am . . . 'twas his horse . . . and when the animal fell . . . .

Joe was pinned beneath. Yes, she knew. Somehow she knew. And she had been unable to reach him through the invisible glass door of her dream. But the men wouldn't understand how she had failed Joe. She had allowed him to go. And she had known. All the while, she had known. But these men hadn't known—and they were offering help.

They'd take care of everything—less'n she had requests?

Yes, the grave should be beside Vangie—there was room. And on the south side, closer to the church.

Joe's personal effects? Yes, she'd take them. Thank you.

No way you can cross the snow—maybe in a day or two. They'd get the new reverend in Centerville weather permittin'. If not, would she be opposed to Brother Amos sayin' the final words?

Brother Amos would be fine. Joe loved the "disciples." Yes, plenty of food . . . no, she wasn't afraid to stay here . . . not with Young Wil and Esau . . . the old dog was old but still a good barker . . .

Best they be goin' then. Lots to do.

"Shouldn't they get word to Uncle Wil?" his nephew prompted from behind.

Oh, they had a'ready. And the missuses were bakin'—only problem bein' how soon roads would be passable. But they understood . . . .

"Y'll be needin' some time fer—things," Nate Goldsmith said. "Now, jest you take them days off you was plannin'."

"Thank you. You've all been very kind," Chris Beth said from the stage of unreality on which she stood. "There's no way I can repay you."

"Mrs. Craig—Chris Beth—" Alexander Oberon said softly, "there are no words—"

"I know."

"If you need my assistance, you will let me help? It would give me much pleasure—I mean, considering the circumstances—"

"I know," Chris Beth said again. "But for now, I need to be alone. Just let me be alone." He bowed and the three men left.

Young Wil would warm up some coffee for them before

the little ones got up, he said. He would take care of her. He had promised—

Chris Beth allowed herself to be led across the living room and helped onto a couch. Thoughtfully, the boy drew a quilt over her while pain tried to dip below the surface of her unfeeling heart.

Dispassionately, she remembered that once upon a time— many, many years ago, six, wasn't it now?—she had thought *jilted* was the ugliest word in the English language. *Death* was better, she had said then. Well, maybe it was— if it happened to the right person. Right now, she would welcome it. Here she was, alone again—widowed now— with a family of children to look after. In a strange, detached sort of way, it was good that the weather had made her a prisoner. Good not to be going to the funeral and hear words she no longer believed about God's mercy, His goodness, and love. If God cared, where was He now? Like Wilson, He had forgotten her.

Did she doze? Or was the dream real, after all? Chris Beth was back in the airless little room—no, she was looking into it. She was in the garden this time but still alone. Joe, Vangie, and Wilson were in the smaller room judging from their distant voices—only she was unable to break down the barrier between them. And behind her were mocking voices, "We be comin' to tell you...they are gone, all gone...we be comin' to tell you...Vangie's dead...Joe's dead...Wilson's gone, too...we be comin' to tell you... you are alone, alone, *alone!*"

The reverie ended when Young Wil touched her shoulder lightly. "The coffee's ready," he said gently. He was alive. This world was real.

She touched his hand in appreciation and drank the scalding liquid gratefully. Telling Alex that she wished to be alone did not preclude this Young Wil. She'd meant she needed time—time to sort things out when she could think. And, yes, she'd meant something more. She didn't need other people, outsiders, in her life. And certainly not another man. Look what men had done to her life. They had taken her heart to an early grave....

23

The Days Thereafter

The days thereafter were white—utterly devoid of color, just layer upon layer of white drifting in, blotting things out, barricading Chris Beth against the world. She felt nothing, nothing at all. Years later, old-timers were to speak of the "Year of the Big Snow" and she would not remember what they were talking about. The snow made her world soft, dreamy. It insulated her against the punishing voices—for a time.

Days were dark. The skies were sullen with sackcloth clouds sifting down their angry ashes to drift higher and higher, up to the windows and almost to the roof of the Big House. Not a trace of civilization remained above the snow. On the first night, the winds grieved over the roof, and then a final layer of ice shut out its cries. The silence thickened. Ticking of the clocks was deafening.

"Are we all right, Mommie?" Marty whimpered. "And why's my daddy not home?" Chris Beth bit her lip and poured coffee for herself.

"He's with my angel-mother," True answered his question. Chris Beth knew then that Young Wil had tried to explain to her.

Marty's eyes sought Chris Beth's in a dazed, vacant stare. "But why didn't he say good-bye like Aunt Vangie—why?"

Chris Beth set her coffee cup down hard, the noise pleasing her somehow in the silent house. "People say good-bye in different ways," she improvised in an effort to explain a matter she did not understand herself. "Maybe it's easier for some to go."

Marty looked at her suspiciously. Then his lower lip quivered, a sure sign that he was about to burst into tears. And how could she help? She couldn't even cry—let alone find words. She had nothing to give. Nothing at all. Her insides were empty and there was rock where her heart used to be.

"Come here, fellow," Young Wil spoke up masterfully. "You know how it is with people. Some stand at the door with hats in their hands and talk for an hour, letting the cat out and the wind in."

Chris Beth saw a flicker of a smile cross the child's face. "And others—well, they just grab their hats and run. Like you and I are going to do as soon as this blizzard's finished. Tell me, have you ever ridden a bobsled?"

Marty's eyes lighted up. "Could we ride one to Portland?"

"Part way, I promise!"

I should be thankful for him, Chris Beth thought numbly. But she could no longer praise the Lord for anything.

Three days passed, each taking on a sameness of numb routine. Vaguely she was aware that somewhere ahead lay an enormous black sea of time that she had to cross—sometime. It was hopeless. She could never make it by wading. She had to swim. But she was too tired...still, she would realize even in her trance, she had to keep moving her limbs. Otherwise, she would drown...and, even in her depression, she wasn't sure she wanted to drown. There were the children, three of them, who depended on her....

Impersonally, Chris Beth picked up the effects O'Higgin had brought. Joe's gold watch—his father's initials on back. His Bible, marked in a million places. And the simple gold band that said once she had had a husband. Carefully, she put them away near Vangie's diary. One day the pain would come. One day she would find an outlet, and yes, then the pain would claw its way inside, twisting, writhing, living there forever. But for now, she preferred this dark Garden of Gethsemane—where there was no remembrance of former things....

24

The Thirteenth Day

On the thirteenth day of the "Big Snow" Chris Beth awoke. She knew she was awake when terror gripped her heart. There was a sudden clarity of what she was doing to herself. Unless there was a change, a drastic one, she would vanish into nothingness. Not like Vangie and Joe who had no control over the final chapters of their lives. But, heaven help her, because she willed it so.

Somehow, she must cross that great, dark lake. Not that she would feel the waters rushing past. She was beyond feeling anything except the hard core of bitterness inside. It was a unique kind of bitterness. Not one that demanded retaliation or prosecution of that faceless person who had snuffed out Joe's life. That would do no good. It couldn't bring her husband back. Rather, the bitterness was directed at the place she heretofore had loved. The Oregon Country with all its magnificence, its challenges, adventure, and mystery, had betrayed her. Where was law and order? Where was justice? Where was God?

In the cold silence of the dawn of awakening, Chris Beth closed her eyes for a fleeting second before rising to go about reentering the world of reality—bitter, but no longer wrapped in a gauze of deep, pervasive depression. Behind her eyelids there paraded an endless procession of indifferent, unfeeling, uncaring people. The drunken ones—on alcohol, power, or unrestrained emotion—went on with their quarreling, persecuting, *killing!* The others sat in the wings watching the parade pass...helpless children...grieving widows... old people, robbed of family, friends, and life's few possessions, but too weak of muscle or spirit to fight. She would have to get away—get away and take the children—before they, too, became victims of what might have been. Where didn't matter. Just away. And nobody cared now.

With that purpose in mind, it was easier to swing back into the morning routine. Almost pleasant to imagine the look of surprise and excitement lighting the faces of Young Wil, True, and Marty when their noses picked up the trail of browning sage sausage, buckwheat cakes, and fragrant coffee.

They did not disappoint her. With whoops and bounds, as if it were Christmas morning, they bounded down the stairs. Poor little tykes! They must wonder where she had been.

True and Marty gave her a wet kiss on both cheeks and with many an "Ooooooh" and Ahhhhhh" sat down at the table with small hands folded for prayer. Young Wil squeezed her hand, surveyed the table, and said, "Don't you think it's a little early to milk?"

"Much too early," Chris Beth answered, forcing a smile. Then, in a voice she hoped wasn't too false, "True would you like to say grace?"

All heads went down and True rushed through with: "God is great, God is good; and we thank Him for this food!"

Chris Beth busied herself at the stove. One good thing about pancakes. Frying them keeps the cook busy.

Finally, pouring herself a cup of coffee, she sat down beside Young Wil. "I've been thinking," she said carefully, "we are going to have to find a way out as soon as possible—" She paused wondering just what she meant herself. Out for help? Or away? *Both*, probably, but she did not intend to mention the longer-range plan. Not yet.

Young Wil folded his napkin neatly and placed it beside his plate. "I've thought of several things," he said. "Some of them wild. Like hitching Esau to a sled—no, I guess that's crazy. And I don't think Dobbin could make it—*Dobbin!* Did they—did anything—?"

"I don't know," she said tightly. "That's one of the things we have to find out. And how Liza is—as well as—" She found herself unable to go on.

"I could try making snowshoes like O'Higgin and the others."

"No!" The word came out sharper than intended, but Chris Beth saw again the mocking vision of blood in the snow and Young Wil's body pitifully injured, motionless— *dead*. The vision passed and she softened her voice. "I can't have anything happening to you—we'll just have to wait."

The wait was not long. In her state of merciful unconsciousness, Chris Beth had been unaware that the wind had subsided. And, while the skies remained threatening, the best she could tell from the little patch of sky she could see, the snow had stopped. The children, busy with a homework game in ciphering Young Wil had improvised, had stopped talking about the snow.

It was with great surprise then that, shortly after sunrise time, there was a thundering rumble on the housetop followed by a soft thud. The snow was melting from the roof! Somebody would get through to them. Even in her bitterness, Chris Beth knew that this was a place where miracles not only happened, but they happened all the time. The warm-hearted settlers were not in the procession of unfeeling people. They were the victims!

And with that realization came her first wave of compassion. The settlers had lost first Vangie, their trusted nurse...then Wilson, their life-or-death doctor...and now, Joe, the spiritual leader who held the flock together. If she could bring herself to pray, it would be for them.

25

Familiar Arms

To her amazement, Chris Beth saw blue sky through the upstairs window the next morning. Just a patch, but it offered promise. Then in the afternoon, the sun came out. The children talked excitedly. A rooster crowed. Esau stretched his legs stiffly and sampled the outdoor air. But Young Wil frowned in concentration.

"Chrissy," he said uneasily, "there's a Chinook wind starting."

"Surely not this time of year. It's usually February or so—"

It occurred to her then to wonder just what day it was and, checking the calendar, she saw all days crossed off except November 30. That was today—the last day of the month! Thanksgiving had come and gone and she had done nothing about it. There was so much she had to make up to her family for. She determined anew that her own bitterness would not twist their souls as it had twisted hers.

Chris Beth realized with a start that Young Wil was talking. "—and with a snowpack like this, the warm, east wind can cause flooding."

With a shudder, she recalled the devastation of the one flood in the valley. Oh, she hoped that would never happen again. Well, so much for Wilson and his rainbows! Let him go on chasing them forever. It didn't matter any longer. Her need for him and his promises was gone.

Chris Beth had thought that she and Young Wil were

109

alone until True spoke up suddenly. "Well, I know what! We'll all pray that the wind blows just enough to make a road to our house—like God caused the east wind to part the Dead Sea."

"*Red* Sea," Young Wil corrected.

"Red Sea, Dead Sea—whadda *I* see?" Marty singsonged from upstairs. But before Chris Beth could reprimand him, Marty's young voice went on excitedly, "It's somebody coming! We're having company!"

Chris Beth ran up the stairs two at a time. And, sure enough, she spotted the distant outline of what had to be a human being! Without conversation, both she and Young Wil hurried downstairs and to the back door where the shovels stood. And without bothering to don heavy, outdoor clothing they began to shovel furiously, pushing the snow from the front door to make a passageway. While Young Wil continued to scoop a path, she went back to replenish the fire sending a plume of smoke into the air. No wayfaring stranger must miss their signal!

Then she returned to help Young Wil, digging frantically until her back ached. It felt good to be so involved, so deliciously tired, and so excited.

When she raised her head, she realized that the traveler—though moving slowly on heavy snowshoes—was almost close enough for recognition. Already, she could tell that the caller was a man. A peddler maybe, judging from the bulky pack on his back. She went back to tunneling. And the two smaller children, released from prison and away from the watchful eye of adults, went back to their snowball throwing. *Scoop, shovel, dig*...nothing else seemed important.

Chris Beth became aware suddenly that her heart was pounding strangely in her ears and that the white world around her swirled strangely like the frosting on a giant, wedding cake. Almost without warning, the world tilted crazily and she sank into the snow.

Someone bent over her, then someone she knew, she believed. "What are you trying to do—give yourself pneumonia?" The voice was brusque, but the arms which picked her up were gentle, warm, and familiar....

26

A Velvet Rose

Chris Beth's first awareness was one of color. Ribbons of light wound in and out behind her closed eyelids like the winding of a May pole. Squeezing tightly. Inflicting pain.

Experimentally, she opened one eye and then the other. The lids drooped heavily, causing objects around her to emerge only in fuzzy outlines. She tried again and something above her moved. A kitten? *We don't own a kitten*, she thought, *so where am I?*

Weakly, she tried to rise on an elbow but sank back in bed with a little moan. The throbbing pain in her head was unbearable and her chest felt as if a heavy weight lay across it. And why was it so hard to breathe?

Above the roaring in her ears, Chris Beth heard the faint ticking of a clock. And something else, eyes closed against the light in the room, she strained to listen—not moving. The sound was rhythmic, soft, and velvety. The kitten was purring! Again, she struggled to open her eyes, this time making out the outline more clearly. It was her own chiffonier with a gray kitten with incredibly green eyes perched on top. Then she was in her own room? And a window must be open. It was cold, so cold. With an effort, she turned her head ever so slightly to the right. There, framed by the open window, was the outline of a man—tall, lean, and clad in a heavy sweater to ward off the cold.

"Joe—oh *Joe!*" The words were torn from her lips.

He turned then and his face was fully illuminated for the first time. "Wilson," she whispered, trying in vain to put the fragments of her thinking together. A weight on her chest. A weight in her heart.

Wilson bent over her. "You have been ill, Chrissy—very ill. And still are—"

"I'm so c-cold," she said through chattering teeth.

Wilson tucked the quilts high up around her neck and reached beneath the covers to feel her feet. "I think we can heat some rocks to warm you up now. Fever's been too high until now—you *did* contract pneumonia."

Pneumonia! The dread disease. The killer. She had *pneumonia! And there was no cure.* Well, she had wanted to die, she remembered as the past weeks began to take shape in her mind. No, that was before she'd determined to swim her way out...maybe she wanted to live.

"Am I going to die?" Chris Beth knew that her voice was stronger now. A million questions sometime, but the truth now.

Did she imagine it or did Wilson hesitate a moment? "Of course not!" he said professionally. "My patients live forever." But his attempt at the old caustic manner failed. It was too soon. The transition was too great.

"C-close the window," she begged, wondering if the ice in the marrow of her bones was from the low temperature or her aching heart.

Wilson sat down on the edge of the bed, tucked at the covers again, and then leaned his body over hers as if to shield her against the cold. She could feel his warmth against her cheek. The feel of it comforted her. Here was life—where there had been so much death.

"I can't risk closing the window—not now when I believe the new method's working," he said softly. "We used to think keeping the patient warm was the solution—rooms overheated, stuffy, stale, nothing to breathe. Now we're experimenting—" Wilson paused as if regretting his use of the word. "Breathe deeply, Chrissy. Inhale...one, two, three...that's it...exhale...one, two, three..."

Chris Beth relaxed against him, grateful for the occasional brush of his warm, woolly sweater against her face. It seemed so good, so natural to have him here. There were questions to ask, but her mind could not formulate them...some of the past seemed missing. But in her numbed state, she could ask only, "Who's *he*?"

Her tongue was thick, but Wilson understood. "*She*," he said with a smile in his voice. "The kitten's a gift to Marty—and her name's 'Emerald' because of her eyes." Now that made sense. And it was about the only thing that did.

Wilson's arms tightened around her cocooned body protectively. Drowsiness flowed through every limb and she slept.

* * *

The fever came back. For days, Chris Beth hardly knew anyone. Dimly, she was aware of the children's voices, but they came no closer than her bedroom door. Neighbors came and went...murmuring in the halls...lighting lamps, sitting with Wilson, waiting for the "crisis." When it came, she lapsed into unconsciousness.

All the while, even when she hovered between life and death, Chris Beth was aware of Wilson's presence—soothing her as one would soothe a child, then speaking words of warmth and encouragement she would never remember. Willing her to live.

The next time, consciousness came with an explosion of awareness. Wilson's high-cheekboned face bent over her own. The dark deep-set eyes burned into hers. His mobile mouth, which could be sensitive and tender, even smiling at times, was tight with concern.

"Drink this!" he commanded.

She tried to raise her head, but it doddled foolishly. Supporting her forehead with one hand, Wilson held a cup of odd-scented brew to her lips.

Weak as she was, Chris Beth sniffed suspiciously. "What's in it?"

"Hot tea, honey, lemon juice, with a little brandy."

"I won't drink it."

"You will if I have to force it down you! You've passed through the crisis, Chrissy. You must have a stimulant and this is all I have in my kit.

When she would have turned her head, he pushed the cup between her teeth. "Drink! Or do I have to drench you like we do the new calves?"

Frowning darkly, she sipped, tried to swallow, and went into a spasm of coughing. When it passed, the hateful cup was still at her lips. Nostrils flanged, she gulped down the remains and sank weakly back onto the pillow.

"Bully!" she muttered.

"Patient's going to live," Wilson said with a caustic grin. Then, sitting down beside her, he leaned his head back against the armchair, closed his eyes, and dozed. It was probably the first brief rest period he had taken since coming home she realized in sudden pity. She had put him through a lot. A shame for she certainly did not want to be in his debt. Wilson didn't need sympathy and understanding. He had made that clear. And she was going to protect herself this time—harden her heart. The tired circles beneath his eyes probably came from the pace he and Maggie kept in Portland! He had chosen that life even when she needed him most.

Wilson, his eyes still closed, spoke suddenly. "Stop staring at me and get some rest."

"I'm tired of resting—and I'm hungry. I want some sausage with fried potatoes, sourdough biscuits—"

"You'll get broth."

When he brought her the broth on a tray, Wilson sat beside her and drank a cup of coffee. "I'm sorry I was cross," he said. "The strain of it all, I guess."

Chris Beth laid down her spoon. Wilson picked it up and murmured, "Sorry. Should have known you're too weak to handle this." And carefully, he spooned the hot, bracing broth into her mouth.

"Thank you," Chris Beth said meekly. "And thank you for everything. You saved my life, I guess."

"Spare your gratitude," he said gruffly. "Except for me, you wouldn't have contracted pneumonia. That was a fool thing to do, incidentally—shoveling like that in the freezing wind with that thin thing on you call a dress.

Chris Beth's breath caught in her throat. "Where is that 'thin thing'—my dress? *You* didn't—"

"I did. Name me ten other people who were on hand to thaw a frozen woman. Oh, my goodness!" His voice took on a teasing falsetto. "What will people say?"

Chris Beth felt her cheeks flame. It was good to be angry, It was good to feel *anything*. But what right did he have—

The moment was saved by a small knock on the door. "You're about to have company," Wilson said with a grin. "Feel up to the 'Children's Hour'?"

Before she could answer, the three of them rushed in, smothering her with kisses, drowning out her weak protests with words of their own. "Uncle Wil brought me a kitten—all my own—and he won't ever sing for anybody else in this world!" That was Marty.

"He's a *girl*, Emerald. And my daddy brought me—oh, wait till you see!" True brought a bisque doll head from behind her. "Aunt Chrissy, it has real moving eyes—"

Marty interrupted her to say that his Emerald had moving eyes, too, and a *body*!

"Aunt Chrissy'll put a body on Minerva, won't you?"

"Whoa, now, you two!" Wilson put a restraining hand on each shoulder. "Give her air and some peace. The sewing will have to wait."

Young Wil stepped shyly up to the bed. "I wanted to show you this." And he handed her a white Bible with a name stamped in gold on the front cover—WILSON NORTH, JR.

North? His name was Ames. "It's beautiful," she said, but her eyes sought Wilson's questioningly.

He returned her gaze steadily but waited for the boy to speak. "It's arranged," Young Wil said. "My name's North—like it should be. Uncle Wil had it done in court."

As long as I live, I'll never figure this man out, Chris Beth thought tiredly. *Which is the real man anyway?*

When her eyes drooped, Wilson shooed the children out of the room then walked out quietly himself, leaving the door ajar. Almost immediately she dozed. There were no dreams, but when she awoke there was a soft velvet rose in her hand.

27

Another Parting

Neither Chris Beth nor Wilson made mention of the rose. In fact, they seldom had time alone. The Chinook winds, so feared by the settlers, subsided before melting snow in the higher elevations. Temperatures dropped but not sharply, just enough to allay fears of flooding and bring bright blue days to the valley. Wilson and Young Wil, with the smaller children trailing at their heels, sawed the damaged trees on the North homestead into firewood and put the rest of the place in order. Soon now, Wilson assured Chris Beth, the damaged roads would be repaired enough for use. They would need supplies from the general store at which time Chris Beth would contact Nate Goldsmith to check on the date set for resuming classes. Right? Right, she told Wilson. But neither of them mentioned what was closest to Chris Beth's heart. They must go to the cemetery. Only then would she believe that Joe was gone.

In the few times that there was an opportunity for conversation between them, Chris Beth asked Wilson how he came to know about—and she was unable to put the rest into words.

"Telegram," he said, "and I would have come immediately except for the blizzard. You know that, don't you?"

Deep down, yes, she supposed she knew. No need to tell him of her hurt, her resentment, her need. He either understood or he didn't.

She wanted to know more about the accident but not now. It just wasn't real that it had taken Joe's life. Not possible at all.

"Do you know the extent of the storm damages?" she asked instead as they sat by the fire when finally Wilson would allow her to be downstairs.

"Bad, as I understood from the neighbors. Probably killed the young orchards. Lots of livestock lost. Lots of illness, too. Some day we'll talk about the pneumonia cases—" Wilson looked pensively into the flames that hissed and sputtered around the snow-dampened logs. "There's so much to learn about this thing—so much I can do for others. It was worth my going, you know, but I am undecided what to do—pursue what I know needs research or—"

Chris Beth caught her breath sharply. "You aren't considering leaving your practice—not coming back?"

Wilson's eyes left the fire to study the pattern in the rug. "I don't know." Suddenly, his head jerked alert. "There's something more important I need to discuss with you."

Chris Beth met his gaze, wondering what could be more important than such a decision. Or, for that matter, how he could consider it a decision. It ought to be clear to him where his responsibility lay.

"Chris Beth?"

"Sorry," she murmured and waited for him to go on.

"I wanted you to know that I've appointed you as guardian for Young Wil and True—just a precaution for their protection."

"From what?" she asked, feeling a tightening in her chest.

Wilson shrugged. "Probably nothing. It just seemed the thing to do—in case—well, things do happen, you know." When she caught her breath with a little involuntary moan, Wilson looked at her with concern. "I'm sorry. We both know, don't we?" he said miserably. And, then, after a moment, "Is it all right?"

"My being guardian?" *Was* it all right? Chris Beth wasn't sure.

"Is there something wrong, Chrissy? I mean, something I don't know."

"I didn't want to talk about this now," she said slowly,

"But I—I may not be available. Not always. It's too soon to think things through when I can't realize—" Her voice broke. When Wilson did not speak, she tried again, "I haven't even discussed this possibility with the children—like I said, it's too soon—oh, Wilson, I'm lonely, confused, in need of...I can't cope alone..."

She turned toward her brother-in-law wanting to say more, needing to pour her heart out. And in that flickering moment she could have. But Wilson's face was closed. And when he spoke his voice was cold.

"I hope you will serve as guardian at least until I can make other arrangements."

"But I'd want to take the children—"

"You will not take the children!" Chris Beth had seen Wilson in what she thought were all his moods, but nothing matched this one. His face was twisted in fury. At what? And at whom?

A sudden exhaustion closed in. "I want to go to bed," she said.

Coming down the stairs, she had leaned on Wilson's arm to steady her legs. But now he scooped her up, tucking a blanket around her legs, and carried her up the stairs as if she were as light as True's bisque doll's head without the body. He deposited her onto her bed then turned on his heel and left the room without saying good night.

Dry-eyed, she lay awake listening to the ticking of the clock. Why was it that every time they were close to talking, having the kind of understanding she coveted and believed him capable of giving, that Wilson had to become another person? On guard. Suspicious. Wary. It couldn't be her fault. Not this time. He hadn't even given her a chance to say that she no longer felt like coping here on the frontier. That she wanted to get away, take the children, and try to start a new life. Wearily, she closed her eyes wishing she could cry, pray—*feel*.

As she lay in what she'd come to think of as the state of the living-dead, Chris Beth was sure she heard footsteps at the door. She listened, but there was no further sound except for the crowing of a rooster announcing the dawn.

*   *   *

The next morning, after chores were done, Wilson announced that he and Chris Beth would be going to the general store. "If you feel up to it?"

"Yes," she said, knowing that the trip would entail more.

"Us too?" True said hopefully.

"Not this time, sweetheart," Wilson said gently. "Aunt Chrissy and I have to talk. You stay here with Wil and we'll bring you some horehound sticks."

True accepted the decision, leading Chris Beth to know that Wilson had talked with the children. She was grateful and would have said as much, but the barrier was between them and she lacked the strength to tear it down. What lay ahead was enough for one day.

As she dressed, Chris Beth wondered what people at the general store would say about her clothes. Maybe she should be wearing black, but the only black dress she had was silk and she needed something warmer. The six-year-old suit she'd worn on the stagecoach coming to Oregon would have to do. Longingly, she looked at the soft pink of the velvet rose. It would look so beautiful pinned on the lapel of her navy blue jacket. Wearing it was out of the question, of course. It was too frivolous. And she admitted to herself, it would make her uncomfortable to wear the rose in Wilson's presence. She wasn't sure why.

After telling the children good-bye and reaffirming that they would bring back the promised candy, Chris Beth waited on the front porch for Wilson. To her surprise, Wilson had hitched Charlie Horse to the single-seat buggy. He had no trouble convincing the children that they were to stay home. Why, then, the larger vehicle? But, of *course!*

Involuntarily, Chris Beth's hand went to her mouth. Dobbin had been killed. Biting her lip for control, she lowered her hand and busied herself with her gloves. There could be no tears for a draft animal when she was unable to weep for her husband. Stoically, she walked to the waiting buggy and allowed herself to be helped up into the seat.

The trip passed almost without conversation. Ordinarily,

Wilson would have talked. He wasn't given to Joe's companionable silences. But today there were no words and Chris Beth was glad. It was good to look about the countryside, to see anew silvered mountains brushing their peaks against a near-cloudless sky, to feel the wind in her face, and just to *be*. Thoughts would be unwelcome intruders.

To Chris Beth's relief, Mrs. Solomon was not in the store. Abe did not attempt to engage her in conversation, talking directly with Wilson instead, and she was able to complete her shopping quickly.

As they were about to leave, Abe Solomon thanked her for the business and reached timidly for her hand. "And if there's anything we can be doin'—"

"I know, Mr. Solomon, but—no, on second thought, there is something you can do for me. Could you find out when school commences now that the storm's over."

Mr. Solomon looked apologetic. "I thought you'd been notified by Nate. He likes to tend to business—it's Monday. But if you're not up to par—"

"I'll be fine," Chris Beth said. "And, Mr. Solomon—tell me, what happened to Liza? Will she be all right?"

With breath sucked in, she waited.

"Flesh wound," Abe assured her. "Now, you be takin' care."

Chris Beth thanked him, picked up the horehound sack and a few lighter parcels, and walked out the door. Abe would help Wilson load the heavier bundles.

At the door, she dropped the horehound sack. As she bent to pick it up, she overheard Mr. Solomon's words—obviously not intended for her ears. "And we're pleased to hear you've been lookin' after our Maggie. She sounds so happy."

"She's very happy," Wilson said. "And so am I. She has made the right decision."

So I was right! Chris Beth thought angrily. *He is keeping company with another woman—an archenemy of Vangie's. How could he? How could he? And everybody knows what she is—that—that—*

Squaring her shoulders, Chris Beth hurried to the buggy. Little did she care *what* Wilson North did!

If Wilson noticed her silence, he gave no indication. At

his urging the old horse cantered along the deserted road to the turnoff. There Wilson pulled the left rein and the buggy turned toward the churchyard.

It was easy to locate the graves. Even after the snow, they looked raw and new. Before Wilson had tethered the horse, Chris Beth leaped unassisted from the buggy and walked toward the graves. Then, overcome by an emotion she hadn't felt since Vangie's death, she began to run, forgetting in her haste to lift the long skirt of her suit. Her foot must have caught on a stone, else how could she have become hopelessly entangled in the skirt's lining and the heavy petticoats beneath? With a little cry, she fell to the ground, her left ankle turning painfully beneath her.

"Oh, Chrissy, Chrissy," Wilson said softly. "Can't you ever let me help?" Gently, almost tenderly, he lifted her and carried her the short distance to the new mounds.

When he put her down, Chris Beth felt pain in the ankle but more in her heart. She burst into uncontrolled sobs and sank to her knees on Joe's grave. "Oh, Joe, Joe—Why, *why*, WHY?"

"Don't Chrissy, don't Chrissy, darling. He wouldn't want it this way." But as Wilson wiped her tears away with a large white handerchief, Chris Beth saw through her own tears that his cheeks were wet too.

It seemed the most natural thing in the world that she should be in Wilson's arms. He held her until the sobbing turned to little exhausted gasps.

At last Wilson spoke. "It's the way he'd have chosen, Chrissy. Joe died for God's work."

Something welled up inside Chris Beth then—something ugly, cruel, and devilish. Like a demon, she turned on Wilson, beating him on the chest with all her strength. "Who are you to tell me what's right? To justify his death? To dare speak to me of God's will at such a time? I don't believe in a god any more—do you understand?"

Wilson took her hands and held them imprisoned. "I hear," he said softly. "I hear and I understand. And so does He . . ."

Two days later Wilson left for Portland. Another parting. Chris Beth bade him good-bye woodenly. Life would go on and she would handle it alone—the way she always had.

28

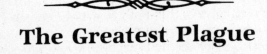

The Greatest Plague

Without realizing that she was calling upon a Source of Strength greater than herself, Chris Beth drew herself erect and walked tall as she entered the schoolhouse door early Monday morning. Her personal tribulations were stored away carefully like Vangie's diary and the velvet rose—items to be lifted from the folds of time one day, examined and kept or discarded. But for now she was The Teacher, the only remaining member of the Fearless Foursome as she, Joe, Vangie, and Wilson had called themselves once upon a happier time.

The darkly-attractive young woman, wearing the typical attire of the schoolmistress, smoothed her long blue skirt and shifted the weight of the books she carried. The severity of the heavy braided hair was broken by the soft ripple of the white ruffles of her simple blouse, framing the ivory face. Chris Beth felt keenly aware of her surroundings: the needs of the children in her charge, every detail. But of herself she was totally *unaware*. How could she know that the planes of her face, deepened by time's mixture of joys and sorrows, added to her ageless beauty? That her skin, though weathered by the sometimes cruel weather, still cried out to be touched? And that her dark eyes had distilled a certain mystery from her suffering? And, most of all, how could she know—for certainly she would reject the idea—that an aura of sanctity surrounded her? Unaware, she passed from girlhood to womanhood—a pioneer.

But Alex Oberon was very much aware apparently. At the sound of Chris Beth's footsteps, Alex hurried to close the door behind her and relieve her arms of the high pile of books, admiration in his glance.

Once he had deposited the books on her desk, Alex turned to her, adjusted his plum-colored ascot nervously, and said, "I have come to think of you as a very dear friend, Chris Beth."

"And I have come to think of you in the same way, Alex," she said, realizing that she meant it.

"You have?" Alex seemed surprised. He reached to touch her hand and looked down at her intently. "I have prayed for you and your family daily. Sometimes it seems my prayers are of no use." Letting go of her hand, Alex allowed his pale eyes to travel over her face. "Still I keep praying... but you aren't looking strong—so pale and much too thin..."

Chris Beth turned away. "I'm in excellent health. I've been under the care of a doctor, you know," she said, forcing a smile. "But you look very tired yourself," she added. "Have you been ill?"

"Not ill—no," he said slowly, "but Mrs. Bynum's boarding house was a casualty of the storm. Did you hear of its demise?"

"The house? You mean—"

Alex looked at her solemnly. "Collapsed completely. I have been staying temporarily with Mr. Goldsmith's family—an unsatisfactory arrangement." He cleared his throat. "Most unsatisfactory."

The beginnings of a laugh stirred somewhere deep down inside Chris Beth—so foreign in these recent months that she hardly recognized it. But the thought of the carefully-proper schoolmaster being in the household with Nate Goldsmith, his innocent-looking bird-like wife who could get her message across when it was necessary with a burst of German sprinkled with French...their countless children...the baying hounds and the half-wild chickens that squawked and took to the air at the slightest sound....

Tucking in the corners of her mouth to keep from smiling, Chris Beth began, "There's Turn-Around Inn—"

"Too crowded these days—which is good. Too expensive for my modest income, I am afraid, even were board and keep available for me."

Chris Beth was wondering how she would survive herself. Nate and the other members of the school board he had appointed had raised her salary from the beginning 50 dollars a month to 60, "most generously," the president of the board pointed out. It was all the settlers could afford to pay, she was sure, considering that there were two teachers now. But without aid of a second income . . . and the cost of such necessities as children's shoes soaring from 69¢ to 98¢ . . . not to mention *clothes* . . .

Alex interrupted her thoughts. "You look worried. Now, you must not concern yourself for me and my abode—or, for that matter, my safety—"

"Safety?" Chris was surprised. Of late, she had caught her mind wandering into the private realm of her own thoughts instead of listening to others when they were speaking. "Do you mean—" But she was unable to formulate the question. The thought was too frightening.

Alex looked at her worriedly. "I must go back to my Eastern manner of keeping my eyes and ears open and my mouth shut concerning such matters—and certainly it must be a painful subject for you now—"

"*Vigilantes?*" The word was no more than a whisper that caught in Chris Beth's throat.

Casting a furtive eye toward the windows, Alex lowered his voice for the benefit of small ears, she supposed. "Vigilantes, yes—and others posing as the militants. And the battle continues between the sheep men and the cattle raisers—"

Chris Beth turned away when she felt her chin quiver. *How long . . . how long, oh, Lord . . .* the thought died away as quickly as it came. What good was prayer anyway? Even Alex Oberon realized its futility.

"It is possible, too," Alex began again, "though bear in mind that I should not be giving voice to this, that thieves and murderers have infiltrated the ranks of the groups. But then, you have been here longer than I and would know more of such matters."

When he looked questioningly at her, Chris Beth answered slowly. "I'm not sure I can justify any of the groups' 'conversion by the sword,' so to speak. The Basque people are quiet, hard-working—but the ranchers claim the Basque let their sheep trample the good range lands, so the fight goes on. It's only recently that it got out of control—and as for the vigilantes—" A wave of bitterness swept over Chris Beth and she was unable to continue.

Alex ran a nervous finger around the rim of his stiffly-starched collar. "I do abhor violence, all forms of it," he said with a shudder.

At one time Chris Beth would have said that the settlers—all of the groups—needed what Mrs. Malone called a "good old-fashioned dose of religion." But now she said instead, "There's no hope until we get some law and order in here. People aren't able to live without rules no matter what we idealists would like to think!"

"Ah, yes," Alex Oberon said, seeming relieved to be back on comfortably-familiar ground, "our society must have rules. 'Man cannot live by bread alone.' "

Chris Beth opened her mouth then closed it. The meaning of the passage in Matthew that Alex quoted should be corrected...or should it? Maybe rules *were* the answer. Love hadn't worked.

"The U.S. Marshal comes through on occasion—more to check on the Indian welfare than crime and what lies behind it, I think. There's talk of getting a sheriff. We can hope."

"Oh, indeed we can hope!" Alex said more cheerfully. He paused to open the case of his vest pocket-watch and looked at Chris Beth significantly, but when she would have moved to attend to last-minute details before the children came in, Alex spoke again. "But I want you to know that in spite of all the threats and dangers we know exist here, I have come to love this strange and wonderful land of yours. It is entirely possible that I shall therefore consider settling down here and becoming one of you permanently."

"We can hope that, too!"

Too late, Chris Beth realized that Alex Oberon mistook her warm response personally. His pale eyes lighted with an unmistakable spark of interest making him, she thought fleetingly, almost handsome in a rugged way. She turned away quickly lest he read in her eyes that she had seen him for the first time as a man rather than a somewhat staid and proper, sometimes comical, fellow teacher.

Mr. Oberon lined the children up at the door and then looked at Chris Beth questioningly. *Where are the students?* his eyes asked.

Could it be that only a few parents knew that school had reopened? Hardly. News traveled fast in the valley in spite of the distance between homesteads. With a sinking heart, Chris realized that most likely it was fear. Parents had kept their children home because they no longer felt safe. They'd seen what mobs could do. They could slaughter each other's animals, burn crosses, destroy houses—no, *homes!* It was one thing to destroy a family's shelter . . . but a building was nothing compared to the loving members inside. One child shot . . . a man murdered . . . leaving behind a widow . . . three orphaned children. Who could blame them for being afraid? The violence would go on, gathering strength as hysteria blotted out reason. The horror of it all closed in around Chris Beth with long, bony fingers of apprehension and despair. If Joe's death did not restore sanity—Joe, their beloved "Brother Joseph"—nothing would. *This would be a good time for a miracle*, she thought bitterly. *Why don't those who believe ask?*

Fighting back panic which threatened to overwhelm her, Chris Beth walked ahead of her class and into her room with outward calm. Mentally, she checked the roll. *Beltrans*, missing. Understandable, since they were among the Basque. *Chus*—their absence was understandable, too, in view of the racial violence. Sighing, Chris Beth accepted that it would be easier to check the names of the children who were present rather than those absent. *Malones*, all present. *Goldsmiths*, present. Conspicuously absent were children of the cattlemen and the sheep raisers. But what about the others?

"Does anybody know why the Smith children aren't here today?" she asked the class.

"Randolph, the youngest Goldsmith, raised a chubby hand. "Their daddy works fer the railroad 'n some people're mad 'bout them rails comin' through th' fields."

That too? Was there no end to this? Where would it all lead? Chris Beth wondered as the day wore on.

Charlie Horse, in spite of his years, made remarkable time going home. Unaccustomed to the confines of the schoolground, he was more than anxious to graze in the North's wide pasture. Chris Beth concentrated on the rhythmic clop-clop of the horses' hooves and the greening meadow. She had never become accustomed to Oregon's turned-around seasons. Back home the grassland would be bare and cold until spring. Here, with the first mists of autumn, the grasses flourished. Maybe if she concentrated hard enough, ugly thoughts of the day would go away.

But it was no use. Marty interrupted her efforts by saying to Young Wil, "We didn't have many in our class and we're scared."

"*I'm* not," True said brightly. "I don't think it's true that the mean men will try and burn our school, do you, Aunt Chrissy?"

"Where did you hear that?" Chris Beth asked, striving to sound calm in spite of the lurch her heart gave.

The child shrugged. "Around," she said vaguely.

Over her head, Young Wil nodded silently. So Chris Beth's suspicions were true. The situation was going to get worse, not better. A great sadness welled up inside her heart. *Oh, Joe,* she nodded inwardly, *I grieve not as much at your dying—as for your dying in vain.*

At bedtime, Young Wil locked all doors as usual. Then, after covering the live coals remaining in the fireplace with ashes to preserve them for the morning's fire, he rechecked each door and window, drew the drapes, and opened the front-hall closet.

Chris Beth, busy with laying out Marty and True's school clothes for the next day, did not look up until she heard him setting something beside the front door. When her eyes caught sight of the object, partially hidden by the brocade drape, she let out a gasp of horror.

"A *gun!* Put it away—put it away this minute!" she

whispered fiercely. "Oh, what have they done to you—"
A sob drowned her voice.

"Chrissy—Chrissy—*listen* to me! Be reasonable. You know
what happened to—to someone we love—and you know
what can happen to the rest of us. Uncle Wil's afraid for
us—"

"If he's so afraid, what is he doing in Portland?" Chris
Beth realized that her voice had risen, but she was unable
to stop. "He doesn't care—" Then, at the stricken look in
Young Wil's eyes, she stopped. "Where did you get that
gun?" she asked instead.

"Uncle Wil gave it to me—told me to look after you. It's
—it belonged to Joe. He used it riding shotgun on the
stagecoach—"

"I remember," Chris Beth said tonelessly. "Forgive me
for being sharp. It's just that there's so much."

"I feel that way, too," Young Wil said, his voice suddenly
more that of a little boy than a brave young man. *Maybe,*
she thought desperately, *this is the worst of it all—what
the hatred is doing to the little ones.* None of Brother Amos's
past prophesies, all of which had occurred—flood, famine,
fire and the invasion by hordes of destructive grass-
hoppers—were as deadly as the plague of fear that gripped
the hearts of every settler now.

29

A House Divided

Chris Beth could feel the tension growing. School attendance grew smaller instead of increasing as she had hoped when people "forgot." The problem was that they did not forget. They remembered—some moving away; some fighting back in retaliation which added salt to the wounds; and some barricading themselves inside their houses. The tension was present in each tone of voice, the touch of each hand, and the way eyes of the settlers scanned each stretch of woods, outlines in the darkness, and the face of every newcomer. Out of respect to Joe, they said, church services were discontinued temporarily. When "temporarily" stretched into weeks, worship services did not resume. "Don't seem t' be a called man hereabouts," Nate explained it, but nobody thought that was the true reason.

Once-happy hearts were in mourning. Chris Beth felt as if she herself wore a shroud of dark grief. She grieved for Vangie, for Joe, and the settlers. She grieved for what used to be and what could have been...but, most of all, she grieved for the three children within her care. They were too young to understand adult behavior. Not understanding, they vented their wrath on one another—particularly Marty and True. Once inseparable, they now busied themselves looking for small incidents to quarrel over, little aggravating ways of tormenting one another. And Young Wil, who had been Chris Beth's right arm, seemed to be less open, drawing back into his former defensive ways.

"The clocks have turned backward," she whispered to nobody in particular one December evening when she should have been thinking of how to brighten the forth-coming holidays somehow. "And in their backward flight, the time-keepers have taken away all that's beautiful from me and from this once-wonderful land." She wished that she had not lost the power of prayer. But time had taken that, too...dividing her heart as it had divided her house.

Maybe the change in the children came gradually. Chris Beth was so buried in her own concerns that at first she hardly noticed. The conflict burst out in animosity a week before Christmas. Marty came running into the room where Chris Beth was trying to juggle figures around to justify the purchase of a few gifts.

"She called me dumb. Said I didn't know *nothing!*"

"*Something!*" True said with devilish delight.

Chris Beth turned from her work. It was a bad moment. "*Anything,*" she corrected gently. "So, you see, you were both wrong. Do you mean this is what started the trouble?"

True looked at her with big piteous eyes then lowered her gaze. Momentarily, she was subdued by the correction of them both. Then she stiffened with anger again. "He *is* dumb! He won't let me pet Emerald—and she's part mine!"

Marty's eyes were bright with unshed tears, but his chin was jutted out aggressively. "She rubs the cat's fur wrong and makes it pop and Emerald don't—doesn't—like it. And besides it's not either part her cat. Uncle Wil brought Emerald to me."

"He's *my* daddy. So take your dumb old cat. You don't *have* a daddy!"

Marty's eyes widened in anguish. And then he went into a rage. "I hate you...I hate you..." he screamed repeatedly as huge tears spilled down his face. "Me and my mommy are going to run away..." He stopped in mid-sentence as Chris Beth sat frozen to the chair in a horror that would not let her move. "That's right, *my* mommy! You don't have a mommy! She's like your dumb old doll without a body!"

"Stop it! Stop it, both of you!" With a cry, Chris Beth sprang between the two children who were trying to tear at each other's hair. "That's enough—no more or I'll send you both to your rooms!"

They stopped in mid-scream—mouths open wide and eyes so large they took up half the little faces. Chris Beth could feel no anger at Marty and True, just a deep pity, and a helplessness such as she'd never known. The children's angry words had stopped, but they were sobbing and hiccuping in a way that broke her heart. Kneeling between them, Chris Beth put her arms around them both, but she knew that there would be other such incidents. They'd both lost people they loved and the loss was bringing out the worst in their grief-twisted hearts. *Wilson ought to be here,* she thought with a surge of anger. But the anger gave way to an even stronger emotion, her own sense of total inadequacy. She who had always been so in control so remarkably self-sufficient, had reached the end of her resources. And that, of all the fears that assailed her, was the greatest fear yet.

Suddenly, Chris Beth realized that Marty and True had stopped crying completely. Releasing her hold on them, she said as quietly as she was able, "It's only natural that people who love each other quarrel sometimes, but we don't have to fight like Esau and Emerald, you know—"

"Or the cattlemen and sheep herders." Chris Beth had not realized that Young Wil had joined them until she heard his voice from the top of the stairs. Eyes averted, he descended.

The color drained from Marty's face. He appeared to be thinking and then he spoke to Young Wil who had come to stand in the doorway.

"Did one of the mean men shoot my daddy?"

Oh, this must stop! But before Chris Beth could find her voice Young Wil was saying calmly, "Not exactly, but quarreling is responsible. That's what our mother means."

Marty's eyes sought Chris Beth's—large and haunted. "Mommy, will I ever get a new daddy?" he asked in a small voice.

The question was startling. It hung there in the silence of the study waiting to be answered. "I—I don't know, darling—" she began.

"And, Aunt Chrissy, will I ever get another mommy?" True's blue eyes turned to Chris Beth.

"That's up to Daddy," she answered, turning helpless eyes to Young Wil. But the look he returned was unreadable. Somewhere she's seen that look before. *Of course!* she thought suddenly, *Wilson's eyes.*

Unable to sleep once the children were in bed, Chris Beth lighted the lamp and read for hours in Vangie's carefully-detailed diary. She read and re-read the beautiful account of the sisters' double wedding in the enormous front room of Turn-Around Inn, surprised that she was able to treat the reading like the tender memory it was instead of experiencing only the agony of losing her sister and her husband. Nobody could have made her believe that she could remember Vangie's golden-haired beauty and Joe's wonderful gentle face with any emotion other than bitterness. She must remember to tell . . . then with a great pang of loneliness, she realized that there was nobody to tell.

Misty-eyed, Chris Beth turned down the wick of the lamp and extinguished the blaze with a quick puff of breath. Pulling the covers beneath her chin, she tried to put the events of the day behind so she could sleep. But the last line she had read in the diary remained behind her eyelids. "We are a family now, all four of us—Chrissy and Joe, Wilson and me—learning to share our differences as well as our love . . ." Only, they weren't family now . . . something was wrong.

30

A Heart-to-Heart Talk

Chris Beth was hungry for a heart-to-heart talk with Mrs. Malone. There was so much comfort to be had when the two of them talked. But it was unwise to attempt a ride to Turn-Around Inn. The valley was unsafe. And maybe that was a permanent condition, too. *I have to talk to somebody,* she thought desperately. But who would want to listen?

The solution came unexpectedly. It was time the two of them made some kind of plans for a Christmas activity at school, Mr. Oberon said. The man had been extremely gracious to her in recent weeks and Chris Beth realized that his consideration could not have come at a better time. Not that she wished to be consulted on every detail as he seemed to do, but she needed his friendship. And she had come to think of him as a dear friend indeed.

They decided on a small Christmas tree and afternoon program inviting parents. But, admittedly, they expected very few to come. The students could decorate. Mr. Oberon would accompany their singing of Christmas carols. Had she noticed that they had come to appreciate his mandolin? Yes, she had noticed. She appreciated his efforts to bring "Eastern culture" to the children she loved.

"I'll bake gingerbread boys for the tree and we might consider making popcorn balls," Chris suggested boldly.

"Here?" But Alex recovered quickly. "Yes," he said thoughtfully, "we just might. Or, I might be persuaded to

come and help at your house. I have wanted to see some botanical collections Wil had mentioned."

"You are welcome any time, Alex. But let's do the popcorn here."

Chris Beth collected her notes and prepared to leave. Alex usually rose when he saw she was about to do so, but today he said, "If you don't mind, could we—could we just talk?"

It was during the talk that Chris Beth learned he had been unable to find lodging and was sleeping in a tent in the stretch of woods where the old Graveyard Shack had stood until the flood waters carried it away. Any day now the light rains could turn into downpours. It was one thing to manage in a tent during intermittent showers, quite another to remain in one. But where could she send Alex to inquire?

While she was still wondering, there was a sudden turn in the conversation. "I wanted you to know how well the boy is doing," Alex said.

"Young Wil?" The report was surprising. In view of his behavior at home, she had feared he would neglect his schoolwork.

Alex raised a quizzical eyebrow. "Is there a problem?"

Chris Beth had not intended to, but before she realized it, she was telling how the two younger children goaded one another, her struggle to end the animosity between them, and her frustration at being unable to help.

"Then there's Young Wil—" Chris Beth stopped a minute, afraid she was going to cry.

Alex was silent for so long she didn't think he had heard. When he spoke, she was sure it would be to tell her to use a strong hand—probably quoting, "Spare the rod and spoil the child." But, to her surprise, Alex said quietly, "Are you sure it's as serious as you think?" We're all under such tension...I for one find myself enlarging minute happenings...and, of course, Marty and True are confused by two bereavements—and in need of a man in the house."

Alex looked at her shrewdly. She knew then that he had figured out that she had revealed some of her own sorrow and loneliness as well as the children's. Still, it was good to have talked with an adult, be listened to and answered. So before she left, Chris Beth invited him to dinner on Sunday.

31

Dark Christmas

Looking at Young Wil's leaf collection on Sunday, Alex said with surprise, "Did you say this was myrtlewood? I am led to believe the tree grows only in the Holy Land."

"*And* on the Oregon coast," Young Wil said proudly, "My uncle transplanted one tree and it reseeded itself."

Alex asked to see the little grove of rare evergreen trees and the two of them walked toward the cabin. Chris Beth washed and rinsed the dinner dishes and True dried them in silence. When the job was completed, True tossed the towel onto its rack and looked angrily at Chris Beth.

"I don't like him!" she said in a tone of final judgment.

Before Chris Beth could answer, she heard Alex and Young Wil at the door. Alex carried several of the pointed, glossy leaves, but his mind seemed to be elsewhere.

When he and Chris Beth were alone, Alex praised the "satisfying" dinner and said he must be going. But he lingered, fingering the leaves a moment, and then asked suddenly, "Do you think it would be proper for me to ask you to consider if I might rent the cabin across the creek? It's unoccupied—and—" He seemed to find words difficult.

Chris Beth, completely taken aback, murmured that she would have to think it over. Something told her not to discuss the possibility with the children. It was obvious that none of them liked the man and there were some choices that she felt belonged to her. While it would be painful to have another person occupy the only real home she and Joe had shared—the only thing she owned actually except for half-interest in the mill—it sounded practical. It seemed heartless to deny Alex Oberon a shelter over his head and certainly she could use the added income. Seeing another couple move in would have been too painful a reminder, but this man's presence could stir no memories.

On Monday morning she told Alex her decision. "It's only temporary, of course," she explained. "When Wilson returns, I will need the cabin—unless I decide to leave—" When he looked at her quizzically, she rushed on, "and there are some extra pieces of furniture—"

Alex's eyes lit up with pleasure. That night he moved in.

The trio of children said nothing concerning the arrangement. They simply looked at Chris Beth with accusing eyes. She would sit down and have a long talk with them as soon as the program was over. She kept hoping that something would bring the community back together. It could be as simple as a Christmas gathering. So she devoted every waking hour to preparations, putting all else aside for later.

On Wednesday before the Friday afternoon program was scheduled, Chris Beth heard Charlie Horse neigh, his way of announcing arrival of another animal. She left the children seated on the floor stringing popcorn and looked out the window. Nate Goldsmith was tethering his horse near the buggy. Something was wrong, she knew immediately. He was cautious about venturing out in broad daylight, except to accompany his children part of the way to and from school. He advanced with a purposeful stride, but even at a distance his face appeared gray. Waving to him, Chris Beth opened a window. Nate nodded, looked cautiously over his shoulder, and ran to where she stood.

"They's been trouble," he whispered hoarsely. "One of th' Beltran children took a shortcut through Judson Smith's winter squash patch he ain't harvested 'n Jud claimed damage—with Beltrans raisin' th' woolly critters, 'twas sure to bring trouble and did—"

Nate's breath gave out, but even as he paused, Chris Beth found it difficult to find a voice of her own. "You'd better come inside," she whispered.

Mr. Oberon was explaining "ablative mood" to a room-ful of concentrating students and did not look up as Nate entered and passed hurriedly into Chris Beth's room. She motioned him to the back of the room and they continued the conversation in guarded whispers.

The masked men had gone to the Beltrans again, Nate reported breathlessly, set fire to his barn and killed an unknown number of his sheep. Threatening the entire Basque settlement. Going to kill animals and owners "sayin' ain't a heap of difference." Then fighting broke out in the general store. Bad. Real bad. A "knifin' " where Barney Ruggles was holding an auction. But that wasn't the worst of it.

With a pounding heart, Chris Beth waited what seemed an eternity for Nate to tell her anything that could be worse than his previous news. Was there no end to this? No hope?

"And it's gonna git worse. Lots worse!" Nate seemed to be answering her unspoken question. "Both sides joinin' enemy camps, less'n our plan works out—"

Nate's last words did not register at the moment. Her mind was still on what had happened already. "But the fire—and casualties?"

"Put the fire out afore it destroyed th' other out-buildin's —some bad burns resultin'—speakin' of which is the worst part of all. Sure you want t' hear this?"

She didn't want to. She *had* to.

A look of terror crossed the man's face. "Three men bled to death—"

"But the doctors—couldn't the new doctors—" She bit her lip until she could control the hysteria that rose within her.

"That's the worst," he whispered hoarsely. "They've threatened lynchin' both of 'em. That feisty new pup, Spreckles, who calls hisself a doctor tucked tail 'n run— not that y' could blame 'im—but ole Doc Mallory sayin' he ain't got long, he refused t' be bullied—"

"What happened to Dr. Mallory?" she asked, dreading the answer.

Did she remember John Robert Mullins? Chris Beth nodded, recalling an image of a plushy man with sagging muscles who was forever in to see Wilson, complaining of dropsy and catarrh and "complications." When reassurance failed to convince him differently, Wilson had gone along with the patient's diagnosis. That made him happy so he came in daily to report to Wilson on his "progress."

"Pore John Robert," Nate said, "he was in fer a checkup when the hoodlums come in to deliver the ultimatum. Doc refused t' be intimidated-like 'n they taken John Robert hostage—"

Through a haze of unreality, Chris Beth heard Nate's plan...a Citizens' Council formed...trying to get help from the governor...hoped to get troops in before the entire town of Centerville was burned to the ground...and there was more senseless killing. Would she pass the word to the principal? First meeting tonight...at the church, safer there...no lights, just come in quietly...and she was to have Mr. Oberon hold the children at the school until parents came for them this afternoon...safer.

Nate Goldsmith glanced nervously out the window. When he had reached the door between the two classrooms he turned quickly to hold up a packet of mail. Then, tossing it on a desk for her to pick up, he left her room on tiptoe. Chris Beth listened, but there was no sound from the other room.

Chris Beth did not look forward to breaking the news of the uprisings to Alex. *Maybe,* she thought, *he will see this as putting him in a secondary position.* He wouldn't relish that. However, when she told him about Nate's visit during the children's afternoon recess, he seemed more concerned about the situation than how she had come to know about it. Which was as it should be. Or was it? Ashamed of the feeling though she was, Chris Beth felt a gnawing suspicion that the principal's concern was for his own safety. Was that why Nate came to *her*?

Forcing the idea out of her mind, "We must keep the children here until parents come for them," she said.

"Yes, yes," Alex agreed, glancing nervously out at a knot of children who appeared to be looking at something in a nearby grove of trees. "But, tell me, does Mr. Goldsmith expect me to attend this meeting of Citizens' Council?"

Chris Beth thought back. "He didn't say, as I recall. I just supposed—"

At his obvious look of relief, Chris Beth did not say what

she had intended. That his attendance would be welcome, she was sure.

Once the children were collected and safely on their way home, riding—she noted with a shudder—close to fathers who were all armed, she prepared to leave the building. "You'll be riding with us," she said gratefully as Alex locked the schoolhouse door.

He turned and, to her surprise, reached for her hand and said in low tones, "You have extended the invitation I had hoped for. I shall do all within my power to see that you and your family remain safe during these perilous times."

Chris Beth watched him, an upright figure pocketing the key with a certain importance, and tried to think of him in terms of a masculine strength upon which she could lean. The image would not come. He was a kind friend. Nothing more. With some relief, she put the idea out of her mind. She would go home. Prepare supper. Act normal.

The children were her concern. How much should she tell them? Nothing, she was to find out. They knew. "You'll teach me how to shoot, won't you?" Marty asked Young Wil at the supper table.

"Don't even say such things!" Chris Beth said a little more sharply than she had intended. How quickly ideas of violence spread!

"Will my daddy come home now?" True asked in a small voice. "Will he come back and take care of us?"

"I don't know—oh, that reminds me!" Quickly, she got up and went for the packet of mail. Six letters. All from Wilson. Momentarily, in the excitement of opening and sharing, the crisis in the valley was forgotten.

Chris Beth only half-listened to the children's chatter as she was busy trying to absorb all Wilson had written in the one letter to her. The writing was detached and businesslike for the most part. Inquiries about Young Wil, Marty, and True. Admonitions for her to take care of her health. Chris Beth read with interest that royalties were coming from his second book while the first book went into its second edition, and would she believe that his research had been mentioned in a medical journal? Unaware that she was doing it, Chris Beth found herself searching for something Wilson had left unsaid, uncertain herself just what. He was enclosing a money order, mostly to help on household expenses as he would be bringing the gifts. *Bringing?* Stifling an impulse to let out a little cry of excitement, Chris Beth realized that such a reaction was premature. She must go back calmly and read what Wilson had written.

> You see, I plan to be there by Christmas Eve... traveling by the new Oregon Stagecoach Line which connects at Turn-Around Inn...slower and not as dependable, some say, but it must be since Wells-Fargo transports via OSL...
>
> Why not keep my plans between you and me so we can surprise the children?...There will be plenty of time for talking, but I'll say in advance there is something important I will be asking you....

In spite of herself, Chris Beth's heart gave a sudden lurch. *Why, I'm blushing like a schoolgirl,* she thought. But it had been so long since a man had said anything personal to her. Then, quickly, she had herself under control. Wilson probably meant nothing personal at all. *And if he does,* she thought primly, *most likely it will be of no interest to me.* Why then did her fingers tremble as she read on?

There was only one line remaining. Chris Beth read it and her elation died immediately. "Don't worry about me. I'm in good hands. Maggie will be traveling on the same stage."

She flung the letter from her then hastily picked it up again. Wilson had asked that she keep his arrival a secret. She would indeed! It would be her pleasure to hold back anything to do with Wilson North and Maggie Solomon... there was soon to be a crisis here she must deal with.

As routinely as possible, Chris Beth saw that the children were bedded down for the night. Then, in an effort to calm her raw nerves, she picked up Vangie's diary. Alex Oberon was living nearby now, so there was really nothing to fear. Removing the purple velvet bookmark from the diary, Chris began to read.

> I hope my sister will remember the real binding significance of our evenings around the fireplace, popping corn, dreaming in a way that can never be undone. I think God meant for us to be one body, the

four of us, and I doubt if He cared how we arranged it. He just sent a band of angels down and wrapped us together with the cords of love.... strange, looking back on it, I doubt if any of us knew who would marry whom! We just knew we'd be together...I guess I never knew for sure how it would all turn out until that bright Christmas Day at Turn-Around Inn, the exchange of gifts—no, the exchange of *love* with the O'Higgin-Malones...then the wonder and the glory of what happened afterward. *Oh, please, God, don't let my loved ones forget that You married us all that night!* I think the four of us said, "I do!" when Wilson placed his mother's ring on my finger and Joe fastened the safety hook of his mother's lavalier around Chris Beth's throat. In a strange sort of way, I feel that maybe it's best I won't be here when it's time to explain to our mutual family about their backgrounds. I would have become confused. But Chris Beth will know what to say, just how much to tell True that makes her understand that she is not without a father and need feel no remorse at her out-of-wedlock conception. She has an earthly father who loves her so deeply that she need not be bone-of-his bone, flesh-of-his flesh. And she has a Heavenly Father Who loves her even more!

Vangie's writing seemed to quiver along the lines of the diary then and there were several stains which all but obscured the words. Undoubtedly, she had wept as she wrote. And no wonder. Chris Beth realized that she was weeping herself. Touched by the words. Touched by the memories. But touched even more deeply by something more. *I just never thought of things the way Vangie expresses them,* she thought. *I just never realized she was consumed by so much unselfish love.* And, yet, within some small corner of her mind, Chris Beth was puzzled by what her sister could be leading up to saying. Not given to deep thinking, Vangie had never been the one to cast new insights.

Curious, she resumed reading. But Vangie continued the subject of the children rather than the adult relationships...Chris Beth would be able to explain to True just as she explained Marty's background to him—at the level of their understanding. How Marty's mother died in childbirth on the same night his father was swept away by the currents of the river the night of the terrible flood... and then there was Young Wil. "She'll know how to handle Wilson's nephew, Lord. You won't have to worry about that. He loves her so deeply that it shuts me out. But I don't mind. I am glad...she knows about all kinds of love—my sister does."

With a little sob, Chris Beth closed the diary. *Oh Vangie, don't put wings on me, darling. You make me sound so strong—so noble. And here I am at the end of my resources, not able to cope with life here any more, and no heart left within me! You wrote this diary for God and me—and we're no longer partners. I can't reach Him or Wilson....*

She turned the wick of the lamp low, laid the diary aside, and eased from Joe's rocker. Wondering at her own caution, she walked silently to the window to peer out through a corner of the pane. Something or someone was out there. Chris Beth felt it rather than actually seeing a movement. Suddenly, a light gleamed in the woods and was shielded quickly. Extinguishing her own light, she stole to the door and listened. Sure enough, there was the sound of hoofbeats. The best she could tell there was only one animal.

She was right, she knew, when a single rider emerged from the darkness of the woods. Chris Beth's thoughts raced. Who was the man? And what could he want? Frightened, fascinated, and unable to move, she watched him dismount and stride toward the door. Should she scream for help? No, no matter what was to happen, she would handle this alone. For a fraction of a second, her eyes went to the gun propped where Young Wil had placed it conveniently beside the door. She dismissed the thought. Weapons, even as a bluff, were out of the question.

Chris Beth didn't know what she expected. Maybe the dreaded white hood of the vigilantes, maybe somebody injured, bleeding, or, by miracle, one of the settlers. Least of all would there have been any idea of a soldier—a member of the cavalry and an officer. Even in the dim light the lantern cast, it was easy to see that the young man wore a dark blue, single-breasted short jacket with braided shoulder straps denoting an officer's rank.

The presence of a soldier would be reassuring, Chris Beth tried to reason. But, accustomed to the all-gray uniforms of the back-home Confederate soldiers, she felt no reassurance. Nevertheless, the man had to be dealt with. So, pulling her robe closely about her, she opened the door cautiously rather than have the night visitor knock so as to awaken Young Wil and the two younger children. Laying aside embarrassment at appearing before a man in her night garments, Chris Beth stepped onto the porch, leaving the door ajar for a hasty retreat. Painfully aware of the soldier's eyes on her, Chris Beth realized that she was standing in the glow of the lamplight.

Before she could decided on the safety of stepping aside, the man spoke. "Captain Ellery St. John at your service, ma'am. You are Mrs. Craig, I believe?"

"I am."

The young man was every inch an officer—cool and direct—not a man to be turned aside, dismissed, or deceived. "I should like a word with your brother-in-law."

Wilson? Chris Beth was too surprised to speak for a moment. "Dr. North is not here. He is in Portland. If you could tell me the nature of this call—"

"But you expect him?" Chris Beth could feel his eyes penetrating her very being.

"Why do you ask?" she evaded.

The captain hesitated. "Because I know that he will be coming and because it will be better," he said in a voice no longer friendly, "for him, yourself, and all others if you tell me when."

Chris Beth met his gaze directly, forcing her stare to be blank. "I'm sure I don't know what you are talking about."

"I am talking about his possible involvement in the illegal practices going on in this settlement. It is difficult at this point to determine Dr. North's affiliations. But I can see that I am wasting my time. You do not deem it necessary to cooperate with the law officials."

"You are hardly the law."

Captain St. John gave her a tight smile. "The cavalry serves where there is a need—" he drew himself up proudly, "and certainly there is a need tonight. I don't suppose you would care to tell me where this meeting is to be held in secret?"

Again Chris Beth evaded the question. "Am I supposed to know about that, too?" She forced her brows to knit.

"Never mind, Mrs. Craig. Just remember that perhaps you could have spared some bloodshed. The Citizens' Council, if discovered, very well may be acting in a similar capacity to the vigilantes—and going over the head of the Army is unwise. If your brother-in-law is the individual who went directly to the governor—"

Fighting down a tidal wave of fear that threatened to sweep her away, Chris Beth said in a calm voice, "What is it you are saying exactly? You sound as if you are threatening us!"

"Threatening, my dear Mrs. Craig? I need not do that. You know already what violence can do—"

"And yet you would resort to it?"

"If need be. But that is different. I am under orders to protect at any cost. And what am I saying? That it will be a dark Christmas—a dark Christmas indeed."

Captain Ellery St. John lifted a finger to his hat in mock salute. Chris Beth watched him ride away, the gold braid of the uniform reflecting menacingly from the lantern. And then she moved stiffly inside the door, closed it softly, and sank down slowly on the window seat, drawing her hands over her weary eyes.

The officer's call alarmed and confused her. How had he known about Wilson's expected arrival? The meeting to be held in the church? And why was the Army opposed to any contact with the governor's office? She had heard some frightening stories when she lived in the South about the soldiers who were on the "wrong side" going to almost any means to protect their braid. But she had dismissed such stories—until now. But what puzzled her was Wilson's possible involvment. And in what? No, that wasn't what puzzled her most of all, Chris Beth admitted suddenly. What bothered her was why she had been reluctant to give the Captain the information he had asked for. *Time.* She needed more time to think. But time was running out. Christmas could be dark indeed. . . .

32

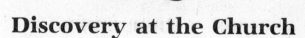

Discovery at the Church

Caution made Chris Beth say nothing of Wednesday night's alarming encounter. Alex Oberon did not seem to notice anything unusual about her behavior Thursday. He was preoccupied with tomorrow's program and the day's even poorer attendance—notably the Goldsmith children. When Elmer Goldsmith, the neighborhood "runner," appeared out of nowhere Chris Beth steered him into her room before Mr. Oberon, his teacher, saw him and declared him "truant." Something was wrong. She knew this part of the world better than Alex and sensed such things.

Pale-faced and shaken, the boy handed Chris Beth a note from his father. She read the hastily-scribbled words with surprise and apprehension. Nate was "holed up" at the church. Would she come immediately after school? The matter was urgent.

It took some arranging, but Chris Beth managed. She needed to see Mrs. Malone, Chris Beth told Alex. That was true and she hoped very much that she would be able to manage a moment with her dear friend.

"I must ask a favor, Alex. If I could borrow Portia—she's a gentle mare—then you could drive the children home. Would you?"

When he hesitated, she assured him airily that she would be all right. "I could come along—" Alex said uncertainly. But Chris Beth shook her head and said that she was in need of "woman talk." The thought seemed to frighten Alex more than her previous suggestions.

Then, gathering Young Wil, Marty, and True around, she explained her plans matter-of-factly and won them over quickly by saying that Young Wil could get the Christmas tree decorations from the attic. "You might even make some red and green paper chains." She handed them the scraps she had saved for making the school festive for the program. There would be no program. No need for canceling it or even discussing it. Both teachers knew and the handful of children had given up planning. Probably there would be no school at all tomorrow.

Somewhat amazed at her courage, Chris Beth urged the sure-footed mare across a shortcut to the church. On the way she passed the steep canyon atop of which stood Starvation rock. One wondered how the earthen walls of the canyon supported the massive rock and kept it from plunging into the swirling river below. Boston Buck, one of the local Indians, had told her that the Indians never went there anymore. Spirits of their ancestors who chose leaping to their death rather than starve roamed the area. Superstition, of course. But Chris Beth did find herself wondering if the Indians she had grown to love lived in quiet desperation, too proud to admit to the Army of Indian Welfare that they were hungry. In a sense, they still stood on Starvation Rock, supported only by the earth bank. A tiny weakness anywhere could send them plunging to a watery grave. Chris Beth shuddered at the image of bronzed bodies struggling against the relentless currents, clawing at the air, as they were carried out to sea. Like the settlement, she thought sadly. Like home. Like her life. . . .

Although it was early afternoon, heavy fog was closing in. The church spire rose suddenly—somber and solitary—as if reaching for a ray of sun. Chris Beth dismounted, not taking time to tether Portia. The animal would not wander far away. Realizing then that she was only steps away from the cemetery, she looked sadly at the silent tombstones, loneliness deeper than any she had known before overwhelming her. A woman alone. *Here!* Here, where peace had once abounded and now danger lurked. For the first time, a sense of uneasiness began at the nape of her neck, traveled down her spine, and weakened her knees so that they would scarcely support her. Maybe this was a trick.

Quietly, she eased the door open, slipping in, and closed it behind her. Inside it was dark and silent. The chill in the air caused her to pull her cloth coat closely about her. "Mr. Goldsmith?" Her whisper echoed against the walls, seeming to bounce back into her own ears.

Fighting against panic, she moved down the aisle, pausing just before she reached the pulpit. Her eyes were adjusting to the darkness, but the movement of the white cloth covering the rough top of the pulpit was so slight she wondered if it could be her imagination. The cloth moved again. There was no draft, Chris Beth knew. The movement had to be a signal. Quickly, she stepped forward.

And there she found the huddled form of Nate Goldsmith. Without intending to, Chris Beth let out a low cry. Nate was injured!

Kneeling beside him, Chris Beth saw that his face was bruised and battered almost beyond recognition. "Oh, what happened?" she whispered in horror. "You must have a doctor—"

"No doctor," Nate whispered painfully. "Ole woman will take care of me. But had to warn you—we was wrong in thinkin' we'd be safe—they come to th' church." His voice gave out.

"Who? *Who?* Vigilantes—surely not the sheep or cattle raisers—"

Nate tried to lift a protesting hand but winced in pain. "None o' them. Soldiers—"

"*Soldiers!* Are you sure?" But inside she knew the answer. If the Army would do this, where was their help to come from? "But why—*why* would they be brutal? And what happened to the others?"

"I was here first, thank th' good Lord. Th' others seen the horses and never got close—never knew I was trapped." Nate inhaled deeply. "They was lookin'—th' soldiers was—fer Wilson. I had t'warn you—"

Chris Beth bent her head low to be sure she would hear the answer to her question. "What has he done?"

"He's been workin' secretly fer a long time—one reason fer the long stretches he ain't home—they's more'n local trouble hereabout." Nate gave a long, shuddering sigh and looked up at her. "Wilson's been workin' on investigatin' money intended fer the redskins—*Indians*—as well as tryin' t' git a carin' sheriff. Somehow the barbarians knew. Now, help me up. You gotta be gittin' back—findin' jest when Wilson's stage's due. My guess is you're carin'?"

"Of course, I care!" Chris Beth said quickly. Then before she could give pause to how or why, she saw that Nate was attempting to pull himself up. Quickly, she slipped a helping hand beneath his blood-matted hair and helped him to rise on unsteady legs.

"Now, if y'll bring my horse around—"

"You can't make it, Mr. Goldsmith. Let me go for help!"

"You go fer home! That's what this meetin' was bout."

Knowing that there was no need to argue, Chris Beth brought Nate's horse to the front door and helped him to mount. Hunched forward as he was, Chris Beth was sure that it would be impossible for him to stay astride until he reached home and have Olga examine his wounds. She would detour by way of Turn-Around Inn, check out the Oregon Stage Line schedule and have O'Higgin catch up with Nate—

In the gathering darkness, Nate cautioned in a hoarse whisper, "We must keep this between th' two of us. We don't know fer sure enemies from friends," he whispered.

Heartsick, Chris Beth realized that the man was right. She watched him ride away, slouched forward with pain, then rode home through the dark woods, letting her tears flow unchecked. There was not room for fear in a heart as crumpled in anguish as hers, she thought as Portia galloped silently over the shortcut which was heavily padded with dry pine needles. It was during that ride that Chris Beth realized with a jolt that the heart within her had come alive with emotion. So it wasn't dead, after all . . . it had only been sleeping. Only it had been awakened by the wrong emotions—not at all like the gentle call of love that had turned her life around when she came to live in the Oregon Country.

33

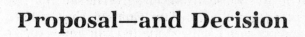

Proposal—and Decision

How much should she tell the children? Nothing, Chris Beth decided, reining Portia toward the back of the cabin Alex now occupied. She longed to share the awful story of Nate's brutal beating with Alex but remained true to her promise to Nate. The president of the school board had reasons of his own for not having alerted Alex instead of Chris Beth in the first place.

"Hello out there," Alex interrupted her thinking with a cautious call from behind the drape at the Dutch door in the back of the cabin. "Oh, it's you, Chris Beth," he said with obvious relief. "I was worried—most concerned. It is unwise that a lady be out alone."

"I know," she agreed. "But I was quite all right, thanks to your Portia."

"A wonderful steed, one I should like to keep." Chris Beth wondered at the tone of regret in his voice but felt that this was no time for small talk.

"I must get home," she said.

Alex Oberon stepped from the back door into the darkness of the back yard. "Not without a light, surely!"

"I could cross the footlog between the two places with my eyes closed," she assured him, remembering with a pang the countless back-and-forth crossings the four of them had made during the previous five wonderful years.

"Then I shall accompany you partway. I want—there is

something I wish to discuss," Alex said determinedly.

"Very well," Chris Beth agreed wearily, her eyes looking for and finding reassuring lights on in the Big House.

Alex cleared his throat in the darkness. "I—uh—am drafting a letter of resignation. The board may wish to accept now if enrollment continues to decrease."

"Oh, Alex," Chris Beth protested in her surprise, "The children will be back. This—this crisis will pass. Just ride it out—"

"No," he said firmly as they walked along. "My mind is made up even if this violence which I so abhor passes. If my services are needed, I will complete the year, but I am not of a strong enough constitution to stomach the perils of the frontier."

"But you will be," she insisted. "We all feel that way at the beginning—" Chris Beth stopped in mid-sentence, realizing that she was trying to convince the other teacher to remain when she so recently had made herself a promise to leave. What was the matter with her?

Chris Beth realized that Alex had reached out and was fumbling for her hand. In the darkness, she accepted his proffered hand supposing that he meant to help her over the path which must seem a threat to someone unaccustomed to it. But when he spoke, the words were so unexpected that she was totally unprepared.

"Come with me, Chris Beth. Let us go back to the more civilized East, be married, and start life anew." Alex raised her hand to his lips in the darkness. After a moment, she gently removed her hand.

"Thank you, Alex. You have paid me the highest compliment a man can pay a woman. But I must remain here—no matter what happens."

Standing on tiptoe, she brushed the side of his cheek with her lips and hurried across the footlog. Alex, she knew, stood watching her until darkness hid her from his view. He loved her, she knew, and her heart ached that she was unable to return his love—even respond to it. Ahead of her lay a future of uncertainty and fear—maybe offering little happiness. . .or the love of another man. . .but she belonged here. She quickened her footsteps toward the lights of home.

34

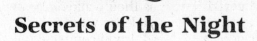

Secrets of the Night

Chris Beth dreaded facing the children. She simply wasn't up to acting as mediator in the quarrels which had become habitual. Even more, she did not look forward to Young Wil's direct questions and shrewd glances if she gave evasive answers. But the pungent smell of evergreen as she opened the back door was reassuring even before the excited chatter of young voices reached her ears.

Marty and True ran to greet her when they heard the back door close. "Come see! Come see!" they shouted. There she saw such a touching domestic scene that for a moment she shed the dark shroud of the day's awful happenings: a crackling fire beneath a bough-decked mantel, red stockings strung along the banisters of the staircase, and mountains of pine cones, ribbons, and colored yarn in which Emerald was tumbling in wild glee. The only thing lacking was the real spirit of Christmas within her heart, but somehow she managed the right words and escaped to the kitchen to prepare supper. The evening passed quickly.

Chris Beth did everything she knew to force herself to relax...a tepid sponge bath, a leisurely brushing of her long dark hair, and her softest flannel nightgown. Then, a glass of warm milk in her hand, she propped pillows beneath her head and stretched out her full length on the feather mattress. When sleep would not come, she turned up the wick of the lamp and picked up Vangie's diary.

At first, it was hard to concentrate and then she became deeply engrossed in Vangie's frightfully realistic account of little True's birth. "Only Wilson, Chris Beth, and God could have pulled me through," she wrote. "But it was worth it, every second of the agony and I am more than ready for my twins!"

Vangie wrote on and on how she was determined to bear the babies for Wilson, recording every detail. They would be named for two grandfathers "which makes everything just about perfect, since Wilson's middle name is *Jerome* like his father's . . ."

Chris Beth had known that, but what about the other grandfather? Surely, she thought, Vangie would never have considered naming a child for her own father—not with the fear she had of the man and her memory of being thrown into the streets. Quickly, she read on, each word becoming a bit more painfully-sweet.

> I have come to think of Joe's father, whom I never knew, as a godfather—even a surrogate grandfather— and I love the name of *Kearby* . . .

Jerome—Joe's middle name. The gesture was so touching that she allowed herself to relax with tears. And then she slept.

Her light sleep was interrupted by the faint clink of a pebble against the window pane. Startled, Chris Beth sat upright in the dark room. When the sound repeated, she crept out of bed and peered into the heavy mists below. Someone was waving a lantern frantically.

Raising the window cautiously, Chris Beth called softly, "Who's there?"

The swinging of the lantern stopped. There was dead silence and then a familiar voice said brokenly, "It's me— Maggie, Chris Beth—"

Maggie? But that was impossible. She was in Portland and what would that girl be doing here anyway? How dare her!

Forcing back angry words, Chris Beth asked quietly, "What do you want?"

"It's Wilson," Maggie whispered. "He's calling for you— you must come quickly. There's no time to lose!"

Stifling a cry of panic, Chris Beth whispered back, "Where—how—and how did you—"

Maggie shielded the glow of the lantern with her shawl and looked uneasily over her shoulder. "Please—*please* there's no time for questions now. They're all over the woods—Indians! Attacked the stage and Wilson's wounded badly—oh, *hurry!* Even now they may have discovered him in the old barn. There was a trail of blood."

Horrified, Chris Beth grabbed a wool coat, taking no time to sort out the dreadful events. Only one thing was paramount in her mind. Wilson at one time had been her husband's best friend, her sister's husband, and he was now the only father her niece knew. In addition, he had pulled her back when she was about a breath away from death's door. No matter what the risks, he could not be left bleeding and dying in somebody's barn. A million questions later....

Lighting a candle, she fumbled for a piece of paper and scribbled a note for Young Wil, not knowing how long the mission would take. She would prop it on her nightstand against the diary...what could she be thinking of? Vangie's diary was sacred, intended for her eyes only. Propping the note against the kerosene lamp instead, she unconsciously tucked the diary into one of the pockets of her coat. Quickly extinguishing the candle, she opened the door of her bedroom and was about to leave when she paused.

Chris Beth did not know why she acted as she did. There were some things which could not be explained, she had learned. But turning, she opened a drawer of the nightstand and felt for her small Bible, dropped it into the other pocket, and went to join Maggie in the yard below.

"Will your horse ride double?" Chris Beth asked.

"I have no horse," Maggie said quickly. "Walked—rather, *ran*—the two miles. The attackers killed the horses. It's safer we go by foot anyway."

"But how can we move Wilson? We can't risk leaving him there."

At the snap of a twig, both women jumped. But it was Young Wil who spoke. "I've saddled Charlie Horse already —heard most of the talk. You two ride. Let me have the lantern, Maggie, and I'll run ahead."

Before Chris Beth could protest, the boy was hurrying forward toward the woods. There was nothing left to do but climb quickly into the saddle and reach a helping hand to Maggie who settled behind her in the saddle. *Some day*, Chris Beth told herself silently, *I will figure this tragic melodrama out—if we survive.* But for now she concentrated on watching the lantern's glow ahead.

Chris ventured a whispered question to the girl who sat behind her. "The others?"

"Killed—all four of them—and the strongbox carrying payroll taken."

"Then it was robbery?"

"It was an ambush—men with painted faces," Maggie gulped. "I'll see them the rest of my life," she shuddered.

It made no sense. Indians no longer painted their faces except with marks to identify their tribes. It was like the jigsaw puzzle she, Joe, Wilson and Vangie had tried so desperately to put together their last Christmas together. She tried to put the pieces together now to reconstruct the most horrifying tragedy yet to strike the once peaceful settlement.

"How did you and Wilson escape?" Chris Beth whispered.

Maggie drew a shuddering breath. "He made me run and he—he—they left him for dead—and he may be—" Her voice trailed away in a sob.

The two miles had seemed to reach into infinity. But at last, a ramshackle building loomed out of the darkness. To her relief, she saw Young Wil pause and heard Maggie's whisper in her ear. "Rein in."

The second they were dismounted, Chris Beth would have rushed inside. But Maggie laid a restraining hand on her shoulder and searched the area with quick eyes. Another ambush? Once her heart would have choked her, made it impossible for her to move, but tonight Chris Beth gave no thought to fear or her own safety. *Wilson!* She had to see Wilson and help save him if she could.

When Maggie seemed satisfied that no Indians lurked in the shadows, she motioned Young Wil ahead with his lantern. Wilson lay in a corner of the old barn, his body covered by straw. Chris Beth sprang ahead of the other two and dropped on her knees at his side. At first, she thought he must be dead. There seemed to be no motion beneath the straw to indicate breathing. And Wilson's face was ashen, what little of it she could see from beneath the blood-stained bandages. She wondered who had bandaged the wounds so professionally. A wave of relief swept over her when she felt his warm breath, even though the breathing was labored. Alive then—but deeply unconscious.

Maggie stooped beside her and reached a hand beneath the hay, brushing it aside, to feel for a heartbeat. "Steadier than when I left him," she said with an air of certainty that Chris Beth found puzzling. "I removed the bullet."

"You *what?*" Chris Beth gasped.

It was Maggie's turn to look puzzled. "Nurses sometimes have to fill in when there's no doctor in the house. I thought you would have known that from Vangie."

Nurse? Maggie was a nurse! So, that explained her being in Portland. Vangie knew there was a nursing school there. But never would it have occurred to Chris Beth that Maggie Solomon knew about the school or cared about people.

"People do change," Maggie said as she checked the bandages. "I would think a preacher's wife would know that!"

The words stung like an adder. But Maggie was right. And she herself had been wrong about a good many things. Well, she would make them right, if the Lord would just see them all through this.

"I'm sorry, Maggie. I really am. But your mother—"

Maggie smiled a little bitterly. "My mother probably gave the impression that I was up to mischief in the big city! And that Wilson did more than lend me a helping hand on the medical terms—I can see by the look on your face that I was right. Give me a hand, will you two?" Maggie raised her eyes to Young Wil's face. He had come to join them and had stood looking silently at his wounded uncle.

"What're we going to do with Uncle Wil?" he asked.

"It's risky to move him, but there's no choice. We've got to try and get him to Turn-Around Inn—closer than your home. Besides, I'm not sure he'd be safe there after what he's told me?"

At the question in Maggie's voice, Chris Beth shook her head. Then to her surprise Young Wil, easing a hand be-

neath Wilson's feet, said, "No, don't let's take him home—
not yet. The Army's blaming him for going over their heads."

In a state of shock, Chris Beth shook her head in an effort to clear her mind. So the boy had known all along?
He and Wilson had been writing and she could have had a
confidant with whom to share but for her own over-protec-
tiveness—of the children and of herself. The revelation came
with a jolt. Well, there were things she could do—things
she *was* doing right now as she slipped her arms beneath
Wilson's limp shoulders and followed Maggie's orders. Then
there were greater things ahead if only—if only—*Dear Lord*,
Chris Beth moved her lips in quiet prayer, *get us through
this a step at a time.* And that, she knew, with a strange
feeling of elation, was the miracle of God's love. His children
might forget Him, but He never forgot *them*.

And a step at a time is how the strange quartet reached
Turn-Around Inn—an unconscious man lying across the
back of a horse, two women—one with hands, face, and
hair caked with dried blood; the other in her woolen coat
supporting the limp figure on either side—and a determinedly courageous youth leading the animal with one
hand and holding a low-burning lantern in the other.

At the door, Young Wil turned to Chris Beth. "Can you
manage from here? O'Higgin will help and I should be back
when Marty and True wake up."

Chris Beth met his gaze gratefully. "Oh, darling, words
can't tell you how much I appreciate you!" she said warmly.

"They just did," he said softly and somehow she knew
that, by tonight's miracles, they were back together again.

Young Wil turned to go, but she felt a need to say something more. "You'll be all right? We couldn't stand having
anything happen to you—and you will pray for Uncle Wil?"

"I will be all right. I promise. And of course I'll pray! Don't
preachers always? I am going to be one, you know."

The young voice which had deepened into man-tones only
recently faded into the night. And Chris Beth wondered
as she pulled the latch string at the door of the inn just how
many more secrets this strange night held. A light blinked
on upstairs and she heard O'Higgin's soft but distinct merry
whistle as he came out to meet them.

35

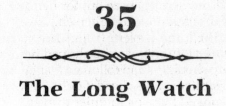

The Long Watch

Unutterably weary, Chris Beth was only too happy to allow O'Higgin and Mrs. Malone to carry the still-unconscious Wilson. Quietly, a step at a time, the two reached the top of the stairs and put him into the large bed in the Upper Room. The other rooms were occupied and the patient would stand less chance of being detected here, too, where the door was locked except for a large gathering. Gatherings, of course, had been discontinued in view of the fear and unrest which plagued the once peaceful valley.

Once Wilson was in bed, Chris Beth and Mrs. Malone bathed the pale face while Maggie prepared to put on clean bandages. O'Higgin drew the drapes as a precaution and asked Maggie to give an account of the ambush. Chris Beth hardly heard because Maggie's busy fingers had unwound the blood-stained bandages on Wilson's head and Chris Beth's heart was churning in dismay at sight of the ugly gash so dangerously near the temple.

Seeing Chris Beth's face, Maggie stopped her story. "He'll not give up. Men with his guts don't die easily!" Then in softer tones, she added, "The wound will heal. See—the blue's gone from around it already where I removed the bullet."

O'Higgin started toward the stairs then stopped. Turning slowly, he said in hushed tones. "Did ye be sayin' the strongbox was packed away by the ambushers?"

"Yes, they took it," Maggie replied, securing the bandage.

O'Higgin shook his tousled red head. "Indians don't be needin' gold—trinkets maybe—scalps once upon a time. But gold? Now, that's a white man's god!"

The three women stared at him in astonishment. It was then that something else clicked in Chris Beth's mind. "Maggie," she whispered, "that was a bullet you removed—not an arrow or a tomahawk—a *bullet!*"

The Irishman came back to stand in the midst of the women. "It's been known t' happen elsewhere—white men disguised as Indians. It's careful we must be 'til aid comes t' separate the sheep from the goats." The women stared at him in dismay.

A finger of light probed at the darkness warning of dawn. Maggie would go home after having coffee, she said. Chris Beth refused coffee and Mrs. Malone's offer to spread out the feather bed for her alongside Wilson. Instead, she pulled the chair to his bedside, waited until the three others were outside the door, and dropped on her knees.

She prayed then for Wilson, pouring out her heart, in a way she hadn't done for months: asking forgiveness for having hardened her heart; praising God for the time He had allowed her with Vangie; thanking Him for the new meaning He had given her of love through her marriage with Joe; and expressing her joy at His leading Young Wil to follow the same ministry "leaving a part of Joe—Your vibrant Spirit—with me forever through this choice."

She prayed then for Wilson, begging God to spare his life, and asking another chance to hold together the remnant of the four lives He had molded into one. "Until death do us part, oh Lord, if only it is Wilson's desire—and Your will."

Hardly aware of her actions, Chris Beth shrugged off her coat and, forgetting that she was clad only in her nightgown, she lay her head on Wilson's chest and sobbed. There was nothing more to be done but wait . . . to pray . . . to wonder if the Lord would see fit to answer her prayers. For yes, Chris Beth acknowledged, she loved Wilson. Loved him with all her heart. She'd always loved him—in a special way that needed no explaining even to herself. Love, she thought wearily, is like a violin. The music may stop now and then, but the strings remain attached forever.

36

Grim Warning

A faint but disturbing noise outside awoke Chris Beth. The light had changed little so she must have been asleep no more than minutes. Instinctively, she knew that the muffled sound on the fallen leaves beneath the window came from soft leather of Indian moccasins. Quickly she glanced at Wilson. When he made no movement, she whispered his name. But there was no response. Without taking time to put on her coat, Chris Beth tiptoed down the hall and descended the stairs, praying that none of them would creak under her weight.

Without taking her safety into account, she opened the door, pausing to listen when it gave a small squeak in protest. When there was no sound to indicate that anyone had heard, she stepped into the chilly dawn and waited.

The wait wasn't long. A tall, muscular figure emerged cautiously a few steps then stopped. Although the man was partially obscured by the dripping branches of a great fir tree, his features were recognizable to Chris Beth. *Boston Buck!*

Outwardly, she was calm. Inwardly, her stomach churned with fear—not of Boston Buck, but of his mission. Remembering his new rank, Chris Beth greeted him formally. "Good morning, chief! What may I do for you?"

Boston Buck, clearly apprehensive, wasted no time. "See friend!"

With all her heart, Chris Beth wished that Wilson were able to talk with the Indian. Wilson knew their ways, a bit of their language, and most of all, the Indians trusted him.

She shook her head sadly and was about to say that Wilson was injured but caught herself in time. "Your friend is sleeping," she said in low, guarded tones. "May I help?"

Boston Buck's dark, fathomless eyes appraised her. "You squaw," he said doubtfully.

"I delivered your son," Chris Beth reminded him. "Your next chief.

The Indian nodded with a grunt. "Buck not do. Evil of white man."

The ambush! Then they were right in suspecting that somebody else had robbed and murdered. "Who? Tell me, Boston Buck, *who?*"

The Indian looked sullen. "Friend sleep. Not tell squaw." Then with a finger pointed to the east, Boston Buck circled the sky to stop the arc at the western horizon. *Sunrise to sunset*, he must mean. Then, stooping, he picked up two small rocks and laid them beneath the tree. *Two days. . .*but until what? Attack? Arrival of militia—or would the Indian know that?

But there was no time to ask. The bronze figure was gone. Without warning, he seemed to vanish—leaving Chris Beth to ponder whether the signs Boston Buck had made were a promise or a threat. She hurried upstairs.

At the top of the stairs, she let out a little cry of dismay. There in the shadows stood Wilson, hardly recognizable in the swath of bandages and rumpled clothing. "Wilson— oh, darling! You mustn't be on your feet—" She hurried to him, seeing him sway on his feet.

"I heard and I know," he said in a clear voice. Then, reaching for her hand, he kissed the palm almost reverently. "They're coming—" But the words faded away. His face blanched of all color. She tried desperately to support him, but it was no use. Wilson crumbled into a heap at her feet.

*　　*　　*

In the two days that followed, Chris Beth refused to leave

the injured man's bedside more than minutes at a time—
even when Maggie came to relieve her. Maggie assured her
that fever was a good sign that Wilson's body was fighting
the infection caused by the bullet. "But praying won't
worsen the cause!" she said.

So, drawn together by a common cause, the two of them
often knelt on either side of the bed. Never praying aloud.
Just praying. Each in her own way.

Between Maggie's faithful calls, Chris Beth was vaguely
aware that Young Wil brought fresh clothes for her, that
Mrs. Malone helped her freshen up and change, and that
Elmer Goldsmith, against his father's orders, slipped out
to say that Nate had improved. School was dismissed . . . and
Mr. Oberon had been persuaded "to stay for a spell."
Words . . . meaningless words . . . except for the safety of the
children! With a start, she realized that anything could have
happened. She must send for them immediately, she told
Mrs. Malone.

"Now, child, just you relax. Young Wil's looking after
'em as good as you and me could do. Then they've got Mr.
Oberon—did I tell you he made Maggie's acquaintance here
and unless I miss my guess, the two hit it off like a team
o' mules! She's been lookin' in on Marty and True—Alex,
too, I suspect. And, besides," Mrs. Malone added wisely, "the
family's safer there—now that Wilson's *here*. Ain't able to
determine how like, but seems news is a-travel faster'n on
foot!"

Chris Beth had heard little the older woman said—other
than the word *safer*. Was anybody safe anywhere? With
a shudder, she realized that the sun was traveling rapidly
toward the western horizon to end "the second day." She
knelt by Wilson's bedside and prayed anew.

37

The Impossible Is Possible

While she was still deep in her prayer, Chris Beth felt a gentle touch. At first she thought she must be dreaming. Surely Wilson had not reached out to lay his hand on her head! Slowly, fearing that the feeling was but an illusion that would fade, she lifted her eyes to meet Wilson's gaze. The dark eyes were tired but not fever-glazed. Wilson awake! Wilson was conscious. . . he was going to live!

Chris Beth could only drop her head into its former position and murmur, "Amen, Lord, amen!" in completion of her prayer.

Then, without reservation, she grasped both Wilson's hands in her own, letting the tears flow unashamedly. "Oh, Wilson! I've been so worried—so heartsick—so—so—but you know how I feel. Just don't try to talk. Don't do *anything* that will keep you from getting well!"

"Just one question—" Wilson began weakly.

But the question hung in mid-air. Maggie rapped softly and entered. "Well, the patient's going to live in spite of us, Chris Beth," she said airily, giving her first hint of a smile since the terrible night that brought them all together. "Let me check him—and, no, not a word from you doctor!" she ordered, feeling first his forehead and then finding his pulse, counting silently to herself.

"No fever. Pulse, normal. But I'm not going to dress the wound just now—or even order broth for you," Maggie said slowly. "I know you shouldn't see anyone, but this is urgent—"

Wilson tried to rise only to be pushed back firmly. "I'll prop you up. Nothing more. And we'll cut this visit short. No need to tell you who's waiting below—not that it's a response you hoped for."

Chris Beth stood up uncertainly. Shouldn't she excuse herself? She had no idea what this was about . . . but from the windows she caught sight of a big gray horse and its rider cantering toward the inn. The man was dressed in a dark suit with a frock-tail coat. The hightop hat and drift of dark beard gave Chris Beth a distinct sense of de ja vu. The likeness of Abraham Lincoln was amazing . . . but the approaching stranger was obviously a dignitary. By the time Maggie, who followed her gaze, joined Chris Beth at the window, a long line of military men in full dress seemed to appear from all directions.

Maggie caught at Chris Beth's sleeve. "I must alert Mrs. Malone and her brood. She'll never believe this—the governor himself!"

"I'll go with you—and help," Chris Beth said in hope of escaping.

"You will stay here and help me greet the party properly—just as you greeted President Hayes," Wilson said in a surprisingly strong voice which carried a command. "Your duty, you know, as my future wife."

In spite of herself, Chris Beth felt color rushing to her face. Hoping that the other woman would not notice, she turned away. But Maggie agreed without any show of emotion, "And they'll need to speak with me, too, I'll be right back." With that, the door closed behind her and Chris Beth was left alone with Wilson. There were only minutes to wash her face and try somehow to sweep back the bedraggled hair . . . not a second to waste. But something of the old spirit was back—the spirit that would not call a challenge to Wilson North's presumptuous announcement a "second wasted."

"Wilson North, you are an impossible egotist!" she said angrily as she snatched a towel from the bar on the washstand and splashed cold water on her face furiously. "You're domineering, you're—" She sucked water into her mouth, choked, and coughed, "determined to have your own way— pompous—unpredictable—" then, overcome by a fit of coughing, she was unable to go on.

When the spasm passed, Chris Beth pressed the towel to her hot face longer than was necessary. There was no sound, so she parted the folds enough to see a look of total amusement on Wilson's face.

"All of those," he admitted with pride. "I am also very much in love with Christen Elizabeth Craig and plan to make her my wife. Why shouldn't the world know?"

Chris Beth swept damp hands hopelessly at the strands of hair at the nape of her neck. "It would be nice if I knew first!" she said hotly. "And anyway—I—I—"

"—love you very much, Wilson North," he finished for her.

Then suddenly, hopelessly, she began to laugh. "Oh, Wilson, you are impossible!" She ran to his bedside, stooped down to plant a hard kiss on his waiting mouth, and said with emotion, "And I love you very much, Wilson North!"

*   *   *

The investigation lasted only a short while. The governor, a mild mannered, soft-spoken man, was far from pretentious. Removing his hat and coat informally, he sat down at Chris Beth's invitation and spoke earnestly for a few minutes with Wilson. He had spoken with numerous others, he said, and Wilson's written reports had been "both comprehensive and enlightening." A voucher would reach him shortly as a small token of appreciation and his services would be needed as a permanent resident of the settlement. Meantime, he would be leaving an undetermined number of soldiers whom Wilson was to use according to his own judgment. There would need to be a full report, of course. . . .

As Chris Beth listened, the missing parts of the puzzle fell into place. The governor himself questioned Wilson and Maggie about the massacre. They explained that the attack took the driver and man who rode shotgun beside him, as well as the passenger, by complete surprise. One moment, silence. The next, the air was full of shots, curses, and cries for help.

"Wilson forced me to leave him and I had to stumble over bodies as I escaped from the fighting, struggling men. Hid myself in the bushes...searched for Dr. North after the slaughter...we checked, but there were no other survivors..." Maggie related. Her voice broke and the governor patted her hand in praise, then turned to Wilson and waited for him to speak.

"They were after the gold—did you recover it?" when the governor nodded, Wilson continued, "Of course, I was the prime target and you know why. Somehow they knew of my involvement with the state government." He paused. "There were no Indians, of course. No local men either—at least, that I recognized."

The governor shook his head sadly. "Soldiers, regretfully. And, while it is a great embarrassment to the upright regiments here who have done a commendable job heretofore, some of the vigilantes were hired soldiers, too."

Again the two men talked in general terms about the uprisings on the reservation...how the funds intended for the people had been stolen and how peace could be restored. The differences between the cattle and sheep men could be mediated more easily, they both thought, now that outsiders were eliminated...but there would be a marshal to help maintain order when well-meaning folks got carried away and deserted the principles of justice. "And," the governor smiled for the first time, "it is my prayer that worship services can be resumed once fear dies down. A lot of folks have been misled, you know, by misuse of the Bible. Disgusted with due process of the law, emotionally they take matters into their own hands and exact their own 'eye for an eye' sort of vengeance."

Chris Beth saw Maggie's look of surprise when the governor turned to where she stood. "Your turn, Mrs. Craig—just a few simple questions in order for us to nail down some of the officers who do not deserve to serve their country, let alone wear distinguished braid."

Kindly, he instructed Chris Beth to answer with a simple

Yes or *No*. At first, she was ill at ease. Then the feeling passed.

Did a certain Captain Ellery St. John call on her? *Yes.*

Did he ask the whereabouts of Dr. Wilson North? *Yes.*

Did he indicate an awareness of the meeting of Citizens' Council? *Yes.*

Did she divulge any information? *No.*

Was Captain St. John abusive? *No.*

Was his behavior threatening in a manner unbecoming to an officer? *Yes.*

And finally, "Now, Mrs. Craig, it was dark and there was rain, I understand. This is very important. Could you identify the man?"

"Yes, sir, I could," she answered.

The governor pushed back his chair, stood and shook hands with the three of them warmly. Then, with a smile, he thrust long arms into the frock coat which Chris Beth had taken from the hall tree to hold for him. "I do believe," he said with appreciation, "that I smell freshly-brewed coffee. If ever I can be of further service—but then you and I will be in touch, Dr. North. Or is there something more I can do for you now?"

Wilson grinned wickedly. "You could fetch me a morsel of food if you can get past these lady guards. Rest assured that your congenial hosts have prepared enough food for the entire cavalry, including the horses!"

After the guest had gone downstairs, Maggie brought broth, said that she would be going home "for keeps" now, and asked Chris Beth to see that he stayed in bed for several days. Chris Beth gave her a warm embrace of gratitude at the door, then turned to spoon the hot broth between Wilson's protesting lips. He was asleep almost immediately, exhaustion coupled with a look of peace written on every line of his face. She bent down and kissed him softly on the cheek.

Mrs. Malone tiptoed in to whisper, "Miracles, miracles, I do declare! And," she added, looking wisely from Chris Beth to the sleeping Wilson, "most of 'em originatin' right here in the Upper room!"

Yes, Chris Beth thought sleepily after Mrs. Malone left as quietly as she came, *miracles!* She let her head droop wearily onto Wilson's chest where she could hear the steady rhythm of his heart. *The Upper Room where the impossible was possible, after all....*

38

The Schemers

Wilson seemed to gain ground hour by hour. The stress and loss of blood had weakened him and he slept a good deal of the time. Chris Beth spoke of going home to check on the children and prepare for their return together. But Wilson would not hear of her leaving. Almost desperately, he clung to her hand and, in his stronger moments, made all sorts of threats about escaping to die of starvation and unrequited love. Inwardly, Chris Beth took a certain satisfaction. So it was possible, after all, for the powerful Wilson North to bend if not fold!

She read aloud to him daily from her Bible. Then, after he'd drifted off to sleep, she managed a few short visits with Mrs. Malone. The older woman was more awed by the governor's mission than the fact that he had dined at her table. "Always was a dream them two boys had, Wilson 'n Joe, t' keep this piece o' the world peaceful-like. Real sons o' the soil," she kept repeating. And on one occasion, she added, "Th' outcome's like Joe was back, but then he never left us, did he? Not so long as we've got Wilson, you'n th' children...."

O'Higgin, looked up from the hearth where he was cracking hazel nuts for his wife's fruitcakes. Holding the hammer in mid-air he said softly, " 'Tis rememberin' I am how in Joe's eyes God lavished a special abundance of lovin' gifts 'long this river and surroundin' wilderness. Used to say, our Joe, 'Now, ye be havin' th' power to destroy it, but only th' Almighty can create ye a new one'!"

Well, Mrs. Malone agreed, it was true. God had spared this blessed corner because of "a handful of the faithful." Best take no more chances. Time to rally 'round, draw closer, love one another more.

During one of the brief chats, Mrs. Malone, claiming to have misplaced her thimble, swung open the slatted door of the front-room closet. An odd way of searching for a missing item, Chris Beth thought as she watched the older woman step aside, drop to her knees, and began feeling around blindly. And then her eyes came to rest on *The Dress!* The beautiful "Ashes of Roses" dress she was to have worn to Portland with Joe! At her little cry, Mrs. Malone said matter-of-factly, "Yes, 'tis that lovely and a shame t' be hangin'—a real shame."

It was a sin to waste, Mrs. Malone went on subtly, still crawling around on her hands and knees—looking and sounding so foolish Chris Beth was tempted to laugh. 'Course a dress so special should be saved for an extra-ordinary time. Like maybe a *wedding?*

Before Chris could have answered, Mrs. Malone switched tactics. Speaking of weddings, there was going to be one of sorts, she said. Love of a good man was hard to find. O'Higgin, bless him, had proved himself. Good man, O'Higgin. Good provider—contrary-like, but a man of moderation. And how could she have managed, a woman left with her late husband's seven young ones, if the Lord hadn't had something up His sleeve?

O'Higgin?

The same. Mrs. Malone blew her nose and smiled mistily, "So 'tis time I take *his* name. Young'uns are growin' up mighty fast. Thought we'd repeat our vows come New Year's Day. Th' deacons tell me they've rounded up a preacher t' fill in till we can get goin' again...and one o' these days Young Wil'll take th' pulpit. Mark my word!"

Chris Beth smiled gratefully at her friend. It was all wonderful, wonderful! But it was simply too much to grasp at one sitting. There had been so much grief, so much heartache, so many fears, tears...loneliness...misunderstandings. She would have to find her way back gradually.

"I'm happy for you and O'Higgin. You have such a good marriage—" She hesitated, then said slowly, "I suppose there were those who said it was a marriage of convenience—"

Mrs. Malone laid down her tatting needle to stare out the window. Almost to herself, she said, "Folks thought they knew exactly the reason for our teamin' up. O'Higgin a lonely bachelor. Me a widow with a hungry brood. But," she said, her eyes leaving the window to meet Chris Beth's significantly, "they was wrong! Oh, 'twas handy all right, but, confidentially, when the good Lord brought us together, we couldn't stay apart! You understand?"

Chris Beth felt herself flush under the old woman's steady gaze. "I think I do," she said softly. "I—I would have to feel the same way." Then without realizing she was going to say it, the words burst out, "But I feel so guilty wanting a *romantic* love."

"Guilty? Oh, my child, don't ever feel guilty about love. Feel grateful!"

She's talking about me—about Wilson and me, Chris Beth thought. But, admittedly, *she'd* been talking about the two of them, too. *We've both loved before*, her thoughts went on, *and we know how much more wonderful life can be now because of it....*

Tears filled her eyes and she turned away quickly, rising in preparation of making a hasty exit. But Mrs. Malone had seen her tears. She knew what they were about. Tatting away, she spoke to Chris Beth's retreating back.

"Time goes so fast. You know, Chrissy, you'll be needin' to think on the "Ashes of Roses" dress. Think I'll fashion a hat for it. There's enough matchin' material for coverin' your summer leghorn picture hat."

Unbidden, there came a vision of herself to Chris Beth...*The Dress*...matching hat...Wilson's velvet rose atop her white Bible. Almost angrily, she shook her head to clear it. New Year's Day would be a perfect time for Mrs. Malone and O'Higgin to renew their vows. And, of course, she thought primly, she and Wilson would stand up with them, providing he was able. So thinking, she hurried up the stairs.

At the door of Wilson's room, she stopped at the sound of voices. Young Wil's? But how and when had the boy made his way upstairs undetected? He must have come in by way of the back entrance and passed through the one end of the front room while she and Mrs. Malone talked. Probably heard every word and interpreted it his way!

She would have entered immediately except that her ears picked up the mention of *guns.* Oh, not again! But the words Young Wil spoke left her speechless, unable to move or let them know of her presence.

"So, Uncle Wil, you've got yourself a real surprise. Well, not a real surprise since I spilled the beans. But I couldn't wait to tell you. They wanted to bring them, a whole wagonload, before you got back. Said laying down the weapons would be your Christmas present. Then, they're all coming back Christmas Eve bringing food and stuff— both sides, cattle and sheep men—you *will* be home?"

Chris Beth couldn't hear Wilson's answer, but she for- mulated a mental one of her own. They would have to be home for such a joyous time! What greater gift than *peace* at this blessed season?

She was tempted to run back down the stairs and share the news with O'Higgin and Mrs. Malone. Then she remem- bered that it was supposed to be a secret. They would know soon enough. The day after tomorrow was Christmas Eve. And with a pang of regret, she realized that she had done nothing to prepare. But Young Wil's next words made her realize that she had no cause of concern.

"Chrissy let Marty, True, and me decorate. I even put up a big, big tree—so tall I had to cut the top off. But it won't show. I covered it with a star. Oh, I forgot something! One of the soldiers brought your packages, the gifts from Portland and they're under the tree. Maggie wrapped them while Mr. Oberon was nailing up a WELCOME HOME sign above your name plaque. She put that up, too, Maggie did. You know what? I have a feeling she's planning on marry- ing that fancy pants! He needs a strong wife!"

Chris Beth heard Wilson's chuckle. "He's got himself one!"

"Is she going to be your nurse?"

"You ask a lot of questions," Wilson said good-naturedly.

"I want to talk it over with Chrissy—but, yes, I had given it some thought."

"Well, then," the boy said smugly. "I guess they'll have to live in the cabin and there'll be no room for Chrissy over there—so you two will have to get married. You know how people talk."

"I know how *you* talk! Now, how are the children?"

"They're making taffy."

Chris Beth shuddered. But then he went on, "Under Maggie's directions. She and Mr. Oberon are going to pull it and make candy canes. You know," he said slowly, "It's odd how Marty and True are not fighting anymore. They stopped all the clocks—"

"Why, may I ask?"

"So time would stand still, they said, and you couldn't go away again. That way we'll be family—and True can be co-owner of Emerald, as soon as she learns to stroke the cat's fur the right direction."

Wilson spoke in a conspiratory tone, "If you want to surprise us, you'd better make a getaway before Chrissy returns. She thinks I'm still asleep."

At the sound of hasty footsteeps, Chris Beth stepped back into the shadow. At the door, Young Wil paused, "You aren't going away, are you? We need you so much—"

"I am not going away. Not ever again. And I probably need all of you far more than you need me," Wilson said huskily.

Chris Beth inhaled deeply, trying to make herself very flat against the wall. Without a glance, Young Wil passed her by and tiptoed down the stairs.

Schemers, that's what they were. *Schemers.* But, then, so was she, Chris Beth acknowledged. If only, if only, she could set a few matters straight....

39

Legacy of Love

Christmas Eve! Without looking out the window of the Upper Room, Chris Beth knew there would be a light dusting of snow and that the sky would be sparkling clear. The bracing smell of coffee and rising sourdough biscuits climbed the stairs and crept tantalizingly through the partially-open door. Chris Beth pulled her robe about her and securing it with the corded and tasseled belt, she crossed the room to part the curtains partitioning Wilson's bed from the rest of the area. He was still asleep so she left quietly and went downstairs to join O'Higgin and Mrs. Malone. The Irishman's voice reached her halfway up the stairs.

"So the wagon be ready for haulin' Wilson home. Otherwise, it's apt he'll be insistin' on ridin' a horse afore he's ready. Doctors 'ave a way o' pronouncin' theirselves well."

"Speakin' of which, what happened to the doctors? Are they safe? I keep forgettin' to ask," Mrs. Malone answered.

"Well, now, the young'un up and hightailed it. Never was cut out for the good life, he wasn't. And Ole Doc Mallory never much be wantin' t' practice anyhow. So the commotion done him in—the cavalry rode in, the good men not the scalawags, and rescued pore ole John Robert away from danger. He be itchin' t' see Wilson fer seein' how damagin' th' strain was on his dropsy and catarrah!"

Chris Beth was about to clear her throat to make her

presence known when she heard Mrs. Malone say softly, "I up and approached Chrissy 'bout the weddin's and all—just kinda hinted there might be more 'n one...Olga tells me we're surprisin' 'em tonight...."

Chris Beth cleared her throat and called with a note of exclamation in her voice, "It's Christmas Eve!"

After a hearty breakfast, Chris Beth prepared a tray for Wilson, allowing Mrs. Malone to load it to her heart's content for the first time. He ate ravenously and insisted on getting up. "Rest," she begged. "Please do—we've a big day ahead, a busy evening—"

"And the merriest Christmas ever!" Wilson reached to take her hand and hold it firmly in his own.

Then New Year's Day! Well, who knows what it may bring? But aloud, Chris Beth said, "So rest just a little while—then we'll go home!"

"*Home,*" he murmured. "Oh, wonderful word..." His voice trailed off and when his grip released on her hand, Chris Beth sat down and picked up the diary.

The little book was drawing to a close now. She had progressed to the point of Vangie's terminal illness. After reading a page or two of the carefully-documented details, she decided to share the particular section with Wilson later. It would be invaluable in his study of Vangie's puzzling disease and determination to find a cure. Chris was about to move onto the closing section of the diary when mention of Joe's name caught her eye. Quickly, she thumbed back a page in order to make the proper connection. Right away it was evident that her sister was writing about her disappointment at being unable to bear another child after True's birth—"a child of Wilson's genes."

> I can understand Chrissy's disappointment because of my own. Now, I wonder if I should have told her that the fault did not lie within herself, but with her husband. Wilson and I agonized over this—wondering which would hurt more, the truth or our concealing it, a dilemma all doctors face, I guess. But it would have explained so many things...including the fire and Joe's unnatural fear of it. Maybe he should have known

that the surgery performed to repair the injury sus-
tained when he tried to rescue his parents, rendered
him sterile...

Stunned, Chris Beth read and re-read the page. Joe sterile?
The thought had never occurred to her and consequently
she had borne a burden of guilt about her own infertility.
But better that, she decided, than for Joe to have known
that the fault lay within himself. Joe had taken pleasure
in assuring her that it made no difference. She was first
a *wife*. Second, the Lord willing, a *mother*. And, besides,
they had Marty whom they loved as their own. But it made
a difference now. Vangie had known it would. Realizing
that this was one of the more revealing sections, Chris Beth
read on:

> It is therefore my hope—*my prayer, Lord!*—that
> should there come a time in the unforeseeable future
> when by cruel circumstance Chrissy is left alone, she
> and Wilson will remember that we are God's "chosen
> people" here on the Oregon frontier—not to wander
> the wilderness but to live out His plan for our lives—
> *together!* Whatever remnants remain must be woven
> in accordance with His will—whether the remnants
> be the three beloved adults I leave behind, two of
> them, or our children. *And may there be children, Lord,
> the twins I coveted for You and Wilson...give them to
> my sister....*

Chris Beth felt the salty taste of tears. Then she sobbed
in silence, trying hard not to awaken Wilson. Laying the
diary facedown, she went to stand looking out the east window at the eternal hills, purple in the distance, that hugged
the verdant valley so protectively. In due time she drew
strength from their agelessness—God's reassurance that life
and love were stronger than death. Returning, she picked
up the little book and read the final words, written she
remembered only hours before Vangie's death.

> God bless you one and all, my wonderful family.
> Know that I will remain with you always. I will
> blossom with the dogwood in the springtime and hum
> with my bees in the summer sun. I will sparkle with
> the snowflakes and in the ribbons of each rainbow.

I will laugh when you laugh. Cry when you cry. So long as you are together! For I leave with you my legacy of love.

Your Vangie

Chris Beth closed her eyes and sat silent as each scene of the lovely days and years together here in the Oregon Country came back in sad-sweet remembrance. Yes, Vangie would be with them forever—like her wonderful, gentle Joe. As she saw Vangie in the miracle of nature, she would see Joe in the miracles of the people he had served so faithfully in the beautiful valley. And it was up to her and Wilson, the "remnants," to carry on through their children and their children's children.

When Chris Beth opened her eyes, Wilson was looking at her, his dark eyes no longer unreadable. The diary lay open in her lap, an everlasting tie between them. Neither of them spoke. There was no need. He simply opened his arms and she walked into them—silently, "paradise regained."